Davo

N.R. Walker

Copyright

Cover Artist: N.R. Walker
Editor: Posy Roberts, Boho Edits
Publisher: BlueHeart Press
Davo © 2022 N.R. Walker

Warning

This book is intended for an adult audience. It contains graphic language, explicit content, and adult situations.

Trademarks

All trademarks are the property of their respective owners.

BLURB

When Fergus Galloway takes on a research trip to a tiny mining town in the far Western Australian outback, he's as far from Sydney as he can get.

Which is entirely the point.

He arrives in Pannalego totally unprepared for the baking heat, unprepared for the people who call it home, unprepared for the craziness and the laughs. And absolutely unprepared for the man he meets there who steals his heart.

Davo is a mining man, as rugged as he is gorgeous. Loves his found family, loves where he lives, and loves his life. He also loves the feel of soft fabric on his skin.

What was supposed to be a short field trip changes Fergus's life. Going to a place many call uninhabitable might turn out to be the only place he wants to live.

N.R. WALKER

CHAPTER ONE

PANNALEGO WAS an iron ore mining community in the Pilbara, a remote part of the *remotest* part of Western Australia. It was quite a trek from Sydney. On a map, I couldn't have picked anywhere further and still been on mainland Australia.

Three and a half thousand kilometres as the crow flies. If I could have driven it, it'd be five thousand kilometres.

It was a good start.

A seven-and-a-half-hour flight from Sydney to Port Hedland. Then a white-knuckle hour in a two-seater Cessna that was possibly older than me, alongside my luggage, and four crates of . . . something.

The pilot thought it was hilarious. He was in his sixties, at least, with wiry white hair and a too-wide smile. He reminded me of a mad sailor, and it didn't help that he flew the plane like he had sea legs.

The landing strip was no more than a cricket pitch—a strip in an endless field of red dirt. The plane bounced and shuddered, rattled, and I held onto the handle. Not for my own peace of mind, but so the side of the plane didn't fall off.

I was never gladder to have my feet on solid ground.

Until the heat hit me.

Stifling was an understatement. I had to wonder if asphyxiation by fire was possible without the fire. The air was so hot it hurt my lungs.

I knew it would be hot.

I had prepared for it.

Nothing could have prepared me for that.

The pilot simply unloaded the cargo by the side of the landing strip and nodded to an approaching cloud of red dust. "This is you," he said before climbing back into his plane. He saluted me. "Good luck! You're gonna need it!"

What the . . . ?

He was just leaving me? In the middle of nowhere?

I didn't have time to protest because he started the propeller and I had to get out of his way. He taxied up the landing strip just as a Land Cruiser barrelled toward me.

Up the same landing strip.

The Cruiser skidded to a stop right by me, clouding me in plumes of red dust. A woman jumped out—work shorts, bright-orange hi-vis shirt, work boots, and a huge smile. She was possibly fifty, but considering she must have spent every one of those years in the sun, I wasn't sure.

She had brownish-grey floofy hair, tanned skin, and a kind face.

"Mister Galloway?" she said, extending her hand. "Name's Junie."

"Hello, Junie," I said, shaking her hand. "Please, call me Fergus."

Her grip was wide and strong, calloused and dusty.

Then, of course, the plane came streaming toward us from the opposite end Junie had come from. At least he had the decency to stick to the far side of the runway, I guess.

He saluted us, grinning as the plane took off. Junie waved after him. "Ya crazy bastard!"

Without so much as an explanation, like this was all completley normal, she picked up the first crate as if it weighed nothing, and slung it into the back of the Cruiser. I carefully put my laptop bag on the passenger seat, then struggled to get my suitcase into the back as she hauled the crates in without any effort. I struggled to get myself into the four-wheel drive, and Junie grinned at me. I pretended I was fine, that I wasn't melting, that I wasn't a city boy way out of his depth in the far Western Australian outback.

"Warm for ya, huh?" she said, slipping the gearstick into first and launching us down the runway much like the way she'd arrived.

I had to wonder if this Cruiser only had full-speed and stop. It certainly had no air conditioning. Even the air coming through the windows was hot. The road to the landing strip was no more than a track, bumps, and corrugated dirt. Holding my laptop bag, I bounced in my seat and Junie hung onto the steering wheel.

"There's a spring in that seat you're about to become real acquainted with," she said with a laugh.

Oh my god.

She wasn't wrong.

By the time we drove onto a better-maintained road, I felt somewhat violated. And there was a high probability I was beginning to cook. "Just out of curiosity," I said, having to speak over the loud engine. "How hot is it today?"

"Top today of forty-five," she said.

No wonder I was hot.

"Keep water with ya and stay outta the sun and you'll be right," she said, still smiling. She gave a nod to my hair. "Don't think I need to tell you that."

Ah, yes. My hair. I would never escape people pointing it out as if I didn't know.

It was a rusty-red. An auburn-copper, even. I'd have thought it was a nice colour, but almost everyone just called me a redhead or a ginger. Or a carrot top. I even once had one elderly gentleman in a Sydney supermarket who called me Blue. Like that made sense.

And yes, I had pale skin and some freckles. Because the curse of red hair on its own wasn't enough, apparently.

I'd been reminded of my outward appearance for my thirty-one years.

"The whole town's real excited to have ya," she went on. "Quite the hype, there is."

If I'd had the presence of mind without feeling like a steamed dumpling, I'd have asked why.

"I know it's been a long day for ya," Junie went on. "But there's a bit of a do in your honour. Eight o'clock in the hall. Get to know the locals."

"Oh."

I had no say in that, apparently.

I glanced at my watch. It was just going on seven. I'd been travelling for over twelve hours.

"I'm sure you know what you're in for," she said. "Pannalego's a mining town of two hundred people. We got a lot of FIFOs, but there's about twenty permanents."

"FIFOs?"

"Fly in, fly outs."

"Oh, of course."

Mining was a billion-dollar industry for Western

Australia. The area was so large, so vast, so remote, that the majority of the workforce worked on a rotating fly-in, fly-out basis. Two weeks on, two weeks off.

It was why I was here. It was why I was staying for four weeks in some far-remote mining camp.

"There's a roadhouse. That's where you'll find me. I have a bit of a store, run the mail office." Junie smiled. "There's a hall. Doubles as the bistro. Breakfast between six and seven. Lunch is noon till one. Dinner, six till seven. Food's pretty good. You eat what Cookie dishes up or you feed yourself in your cabin."

When the brief said meals were provided, I hadn't realised it was a cafeteria situation.

"We get food deliveries and mail Mondays and Fridays," she added. "The joys of being one of the most remote towns in the country, huh?"

When I'd applied for this position, remote was the deciding factor. I hadn't realised just what that meant. We were literally hundreds of kilometres from anywhere, surrounded by red, baking desert. I tried smiling, but it wasn't easy when my face was melting.

She shot me a serious look. "And you know we're a dry town, right?"

Dry, as in the middle of the desert, yes. But also dry as in no alcohol. It made sense that far-remote towns, with a ninety-seven per cent male population, didn't drink. The fact they also operated gigantic, expensive machinery for a living was also a factor, but the town itself was basically owned by the mining company. But loneliness, isolation, and alcohol rarely mixed well. Especially when coupled with high levels of testosterone, frustration, and brain-melting heat.

Another reason I was here. The psychological factors, not the no alcohol.

"Yes, I know. I never was a big drinker."

"You'll want to stick to water out here anyway," she said, back to smiling. "Though I recommend you boil it first."

Oh good.

Then we drove into town. And I could use that term very loosely. Pannalego was a *town*, yes, but it was really more of a camp. There were rows of government-style cabins, perhaps one hundred and fifty, that looked more like a caravan park, which appeared to have every surface covered with red dust.

The roadhouse was a large rectangular building with a huge undercover area with petrol bowsers, and there were signs for Coca-Cola. It didn't really need an explanation. "That's the hall," Junie explained, pointing to the equally large rectangular building next to the roadhouse. The hall had a row of square tinted windows along the front, a ramp up to the door. All the buildings were tin, specially insulated to keep out the heat. Or so I'd read.

"The doc is here on the corner, and all the permanents are along the front two rows," Junie said. "The FIFOs take what's left. They change cabins anyway, but the locals keep their own." She turned down the first little street and pulled up to the front cabin in the second row. "Oh, and that's the laundry over there," she said, pointing to a long rectangular building behind the hall. "Clothes on the line will dry in about five minutes."

I guessed that was not an exaggeration.

"And this is you," she said, pulling the Cruiser to a stop. "All the communal buildings are at the front of town, so you're nice and close to everything."

She looked at my hands then, and I realised I was clutching my laptop bag a little too tight.

Don't panic. Don't panic. You signed up for this. Four weeks. Just four . . .

"Come on," she said, getting out. "Or you'll be late to your own welcoming party."

Chapter Two

Junie unlocked the front door, handed me my keys, and came back for my suitcase. "You'll wanna open the windows, probably dust a bit. Let the water run for a while to clear your pipes. I turned yer fridge on this morning. Oh, and you'll wanna keep all open food and any fruit in the fridge."

I wiped dirt-red sweat from my brow. "Yeah, this heat... phew."

"Oh." She grimaced. "Well, yeah. But the goannas can open the screen doors. Helps to keep 'em locked even when you're home. Keeps the pesky buggers out."

Goannas...

The dinosaur-lizards that grew up to two metres long, with raptor talons? They could open doors?

She laughed at my expression. "Each house has a UH radio. Channel five is the local spot for anything you need. You get a snake, just holler on channel five and someone'll come and take care of it for ya."

Don't panic.

Do not panic.

Do not . . .

"Right, then. I'll leave you to get settled," she said. She pointed to the hall as she got back in her Cruiser. "Eight o'clock. Don't forget."

I walked into my 'home' in a daze. In a steaming, scorching-hot daze. It was like a holiday cabin you'd find in a caravan park. A small kitchen, a small round table with three chairs, a bathroom, and one bedroom. And a small portable air conditioner, which Junie must have turned on the same time as the fridge.

It was much cooler inside and perfectly adequate. Yellows and blues, pale lino floor. There was even a toaster and a kettle. A fridge, which, upon opening, I could see was indeed working, and there was even a bowl inside with one apple, a banana, and a mandarin.

I should have thanked Junie for thinking to turn it on for me. I didn't even thank her for picking me up from the . . . airstrip. It certainly wasn't an airport.

A pile of neatly folded linens sat on the bed, towels in the bathroom . . . The idea of a cold shower had never been so appealing. I switched on all the ceiling fans and opened the windows a little to let out the musty smell. The place would need a good dusting, for sure.

But first a shower.

I remembered to lock the door—god forbid a freaking goanna helped itself inside—went into the bathroom, stripped naked, and turned the cold water on.

It was so hot it scalded me, and it ran red. The dust swirled down the drain as I waited and waited for the water to get any cooler.

It didn't.

How could the cold water be hot?

Lord.

But at least it washed the dirt and sweat off my body. It also made me sweat, which was the opposite of what I'd wanted. It was the quickest shower of my life.

Checking my luggage, I realised packing mostly work clothes of trousers and long-sleeve shirts was a grave mistake, but I had little choice but to wear them. I had a few pairs of gym shorts, but I could hardly wear those to meet the locals.

I wanted to make a good impression at my albeit unexpected welcoming party. I was here to conduct a study on the human aspects of the mining industry. I'd expected to be met with indifference, not a *welcoming* party.

If I was spending the next four weeks with these people, I needed to be professional from the first day. I didn't need them to like me, per se. I just needed them to be honest and maybe not hate me.

Maybe a welcoming party would be a good idea?

So just on eight, I went back out into the dreadful heat, across the narrow road and up the ramp, and into the hall. It was a huge open room filled with tables and chairs, a kitchen behind a service counter at one end, a small stage at the other. Noticeboards filled with announcements and photos hung on the wall.

And about thirty people, all wearing fluoro-orange hi-vis workwear covered with red dust, stopped and stared at me.

Silence filled the huge room.

Until Junie appeared and ushered me in. "Come in, come in."

I was thankful for a familiar face as a distraction from everyone staring. "I never got to thank you earlier," I said, shaking her hand again.

"Don't mention it." She waved me off. Then to my absolute horror, she cleared her throat and boomed, "If I could have your attention, please."

Everyone formed a kind of circle around us, all eyes on me.

Oh, good heavens.

"There's a new guy in town," Junie said. "We'll let him tell us a bit about himself."

I waved like an idiot, then shoved my hand into my pocket so I didn't do that again. "Uh, hi," I began, my voice cracking. I tried again. "My name is Fergus Galloway. I'm from the University of Sydney Central. I'm here to learn about the human aspects of the mining industry and how remote living impacts those who work here."

They stared as if I'd spoken a different language.

Maybe that sounded like a work speech? So I added a smile. And I wanted them to know I wasn't a spy. "I'm not employed by the mining industry or the government. It's an independent study."

They still stared.

"I'm excited to be here. Well, except for the heat," I tacked on, aiming for at least one smile.

Nada.

Boy, these were a tough crowd.

"We have two heat settings here, mate," one man in the back of the crowd said. "We have hot and fucking hot."

Everyone laughed, and I played along. "I'm guessing today's the latter."

The ice seemed to have been broken, because another man came forward and offered me his huge, hard hand. He would have been about fifty-five. Big guy, seemed friendly. "Name's Bill. I run the roadhouse with my wife, Junie. Not gonna lie, when we heard some scientific researcher was coming along, I pictured someone a few years older."

Ah.

Before I could reply, another man interrupted. "Name's Chappy."

And then another. And another and another.

Chappy was a pastor of sorts. Did readings on Sundays if I was interested. My religion didn't matter because apparently, he covered them all.

Truck was the guy to go to for haircuts. JC would read books over the UH radio on Mondays and Thursdays at eight o'clock. Channel five, *be sure to listen*. Bronnie held bingo nights on Wednesdays. Gibbo could fix any appliance. Creepy made art out of recyclables, *so if I could please keep any recyclable objects aside, that'd be much appreciated*.

Not sure I wanted to know why they called him Creepy.

And Cookie, resident cook, if his name didn't give that away. He came out from the kitchen holding a slab cake, which I got the distinct impression was the real reason people were here, because suddenly everyone was way less interested in me and more interested in getting a plate.

Junie handed me a cup of lemon water and a paper plate with a slice of cake on it. "Thank you. I wasn't expecting a welcome party. It was a lovely surprise."

Well, it was lovely and sweet, but also a little horrifying and awkward.

She gave me a huge smile. "You'll settle in just fine," she said. "Great little town, it is. The permanents are real good souls. A little unconventional, but do anything for ya."

Unconventional was one way to put it. Eccentric was another. Being cut off from society was—

"Oh, Davo," Junie said to a newcomer. "Grab yourself some cake before it's all gone."

I bit into my cake and glanced at the guy who'd just arrived . . . and almost forgot to chew.

He had short, dark-blond hair and the body of an athlete: muscular and fit. He wore work boots like everyone else here, a too-tight white tee shirt, and a pink tiered skirt.

My first thought was that it was a joke. That someone, somehow, had found out I was gay, and this was a terrible piss-take, a mockery, and I waited for the jokes. For the pointing and the laughing and the insults.

But no one looked twice at him, except to say hello. Someone asked him about a drive shaft something or other. He ate his cake with grease-stained hands. He talked to someone else about the oil pressure of some machine, and he wiped his hands on a serviette and sipped his drink, engrossed in conversation.

No one raised an eyebrow.

He clearly wore a skirt often. I could see now he had a bit of stubble, blue eyes, and dark eyelashes. He was both handsome and pretty.

So handsome, and so very pretty.

Then Junie called him over. "Davo, this is the research guy we were told about."

I looked at both my full hands. Jeez. I put the lemon water down, then the plate, and had to wipe the icing off my hand onto my shirt.

Like a heathen.

"Nice to meet you," I said. "Davo, was it? My name is Fergus. Um, Fergus Galloway."

On a scale of one to mortifying, that was an eleven.

Good one, Fergus.

He held my gaze and my hand for a beat too long. "Nice to meet you too."

I was stuck for a moment, rendered speechless. He was possibly the most handsome and beautiful man I'd ever seen.

"Research, huh?"

He hadn't been here for my earlier explanation, brief as it was, so I repeated it.

"Yeah. I write unbiased reports that go to the mining corps and various government departments, irrespective of what they want to hear, so they can take into consideration the effects this kind of work has on the people who live out here. I'm not paid by the mining giants or the government," I said. "I'm not here for the ecological sustainability or the financial impacts of mining. I'm here for the human impact. My background is human studies and social anthropology."

I didn't want to get too bogged down in details in case they all decided they'd rather not speak to me, but I wanted them to also know I wasn't some hack. Not that it mattered, apparently, because none of them seemed to care one bit.

Davo smiled as he sipped his drink, and he nodded to my hair. "Might wanna stay out of the sun with that complexion."

He was going to joke about my appearance when he was wearing a skirt?

Okay then.

His eyes sparkled with humour, his gaze gripped onto me, refusing to let me go.

You're not here for this, Fergus.

No personal relations with the people of your research report, Fergus. No matter how cute they are with a killer smile and pretty skirt, no matter how he looks at you.

But then he cracked a crooked smile. Perfect teeth,

perfect lips, perfectly uneven smile. He raised an eyebrow, a brief flicker of acknowledgement passing between us, from one gay man to another.

And just like that my brain pulled on the handbrake and, along with my good judgement, went careening off the road.

Chapter Three

Later that night, when the party was over and I'd gone back to my cabin, I lay in my bed, atop the sheets and under the ceiling fan, still thinking about him.

He'd left me speechless.

That hadn't happened in . . . well, ever.

I tried to get him out of my mind—the boots, the smirk, the tight shirt, the pretty skirt.

God, the skirt. He had the body of a footballer, grease-stained hands, work boots, and a pretty skirt.

It was an Achilles heel I didn't know I had, apparently.

I tried to not think about him most of the sleepless night. And the next morning while I drank my breakfast coffee. And while I opened up my laptop and report.

It was barely 8:00am, already forty degrees, but I was determined to not think of Davo and his incredible legs while I worked. I'd arranged to meet with the local, and only, doctor in town first thing.

I would imagine a town like Pannalego had many essential hub workers that kept the community running, and the doctor would be a good place to start. He'd kindly agreed to meet me before his first patient.

Doctor Stan Wakely was a tall, wiry man in his sixties, at a guess. He had long grey hair pulled back in a thin pony-tail. His glasses had a band of sticky tape on the hinge of the arm. He wore shorts and sandals and an old *Jaws* shirt that I had no doubt he'd bought brand new back in the 1980s.

His doctor's office was a cabin like all others, except the bedroom was his examination room, the small living area his waiting room.

"Thank you for agreeing to see me," I said.

He took his cup of tea and showed me into the examination room. He sat at his desk, and I sat in the patient chair.

"I have five minutes," he said, giving me a prompting nod.

Right. "Yes, I'm sure you're very busy," I agreed, "being the only doctor in town. How did you find yourself here?"

"I've been here for ten years. Came from Darwin. Just what are you trying to find in this report of yours?"

"How the remoteness and isolation in one of the harshest environments on earth affects the people who live and work here," I replied. "That's the simplified answer."

"What are you hoping to find?"

"I'm not hoping to find anything. My report will be without bias."

He stared at me through his glasses and blinked. "Hm."

I needed to redirect the conversation. "How is your work here any different from when you worked in Darwin?"

"My job here is mostly treating small ailments, main-taining prescriptions, and doing mandatory physicals. Any emergencies are choppered to Port Hedland." He shrugged. "You have to understand, the people here are tougher than most. Saw a guy once put a metal rod through his hand. He just pulled it out, poured some diesel on it, and kept on working."

"Oh god."

Doctor Wakely sipped his tea. "Resources aren't difficult to get, but they can take time to get in. We keep no hard drugs here, just paracetamol, ibuprofen, and some basic antibiotics. We had some antivenin once, but it went out of date."

Oh my god!

"What if someone gets bitten?"

He grimaced. "Well, for the snakes you find out this way, the chopper wouldn't get here in time anyway. So my advice is just don't get bitten."

Holy hell.

"Sound advice," I said, trying to think of the ways I could stay here for four weeks and not leave my cabin.

"Anything else?"

"Ah, yes," I replied. "How does the government or the mining company deal with mental health out here?"

He laughed. "They don't. We do. We have coping mechanisms. We made our own community and we made it work. You'd think the permanent residents here would be around the twist, but if you ask me, it's the FIFOs who struggle. They still have a life outside of here, and it's all they want to get back to. But us permanents, we do just fine. You might think we're stuck out here, forced to work in such extreme conditions that you think are unbearable, but we choose this. This is our home."

"What's your coping mechanism?" I asked. "What do you do in your downtime?"

He suddenly became animated, his eyes lit up, his smile widened. He jumped up and went to what I'd thought was a broom cupboard, where he pulled out a . . . a metal detector?

"She's the Aurum 2000," he whispered, holding it as if it were the Holy Grail. "Isn't she beautiful?"

The handle was wrapped in duct tape, covered in sweat and red dirt. The entire thing had scratches, and the disc thing at the bottom had more dents than my first car.

"Yep, she's a beauty," I said, now questioning this man's sanity. The wild look in his eyes was a concern. "What do you look for?"

He whipped his gaze to mine. "Gold."

Okaaaay. I suddenly felt like Bilbo in Smaug's lair. I wasn't brave enough to ask if he'd ever found any. "Wow. That's excellent," I said instead. "Thank you for your time. I know you're busy, so I really appreciate your time."

He put his *precious* back in its cupboard and closed it. "You're here for a few weeks, right?"

I nodded. "Four weeks."

"You might want to come out detecting with me one day."

After what he'd just told me about the antivenin situation, that was highly unlikely to ever happen. "Ah, thanks. I'm sure I'll see you around."

He opened the door out into the waiting room, and it surprised me to see it full.

And not just with people.

"Morning, Doc," one man said brightly. He was holding a tabby cat. "Maisie's off her food. I was hoping you could check her over."

The doctor also tended to animals? "Ummm, it's a cat!" I said, not really meaning to say it out loud.

He looked at me like *I* was the strange one. "That's correct."

I noticed then that another guy was holding a large lizard. I tried to keep my voice calm. "What is that?"

"This is Lizzy Taylor." He held it up in both hands. "She's got a sore eye."

What the ... ?

One lady was sitting, reading something on her phone. She didn't have an animal with her, so that was a good thing.

I looked to the next guy. He had a dirty bandage around his palm and took my staring at it as a cue. "I put a piece of tin through me hand a coupla days ago. It's not lookin' too good."

"Okay," Doctor Wakely said, implying maybe he'd be first.

But then a tall guy who was standing awkwardly in the corner made a whining noise. He had no outward injury and he wasn't holding an animal, which was a relief. Doctor Wakely gestured to a vacant chair. "Jeff? Would you like to take a seat? I'll be with you in a sec."

Jeff's eyes went wide and he blushed, silent for a long beat. "I'd, uh, I'd rather not sit down, thanks."

Oh dear.

Ouch.

With a nod to the standing man, the doctor opened the door wider in invitation. "You first then."

I was just about to leave when Truck came in, one of the men I'd met at my welcoming party the night before. He had a sulphur-crested cockatoo perched on his forearm.

"Oh, hello again," I said. To Truck, not the bird.

The large bird squawked, his yellow crest perked right up. "What the fuck do you want?"

I was stunned.

Truck laughed. "This is Hooker. He has no manners, sorry."

I was still startled at the language and the decibels with which it was delivered. I looked around the waiting room, so very confused. "Does, uh, is the good doctor also a vet?"

Truck laughed. "Nah. Could be, though. He'll look over the resident animals one day a month. Today's the day."

"What the fuck do you want?" Hooker screeched again, this time at Maisie the cat. Maisie looked horrified, her expression probably matching mine. I'd imagine being cussed at by a huge screeching bird wasn't doing her upset tummy any favours.

"You behave yourself," Truck hissed at Hooker. "Or you'll go back in your cage."

Hooker then proceeded to bob up and down, the way birds do, and screech, "No, no, no, no, no, no, no, no, no."

Truck sighed. "He belonged to old Wally. Raised him from a baby, and you don't have to guess what Wally's language was like. Crazy old bastard. Anyway, Wally passed away a few months back now, and Hooker couldn't be released because he doesn't know how to be a bird. He couldn't go to some poor, unsuspecting wildlife park because of the language."

Hooker let rip, right on cue, "The fuck, the fuck, the fuck, the fuck, the fuck."

"So me and Bronnie took him," Truck said over the noise. "Old Wally told us he liked bark. That'd calm him down, and he was always getting some kind of sticks and branches from trees. We've tried different kinds, but he just shreds 'em. Makes a helluva mess."

"Some tree bark has certain oils in it," the lizard guy said. "Cockatoos love red cedar, apparently. Will eat a whole house if you let him."

Truck sighed. "Figures. Destructive bloody things." He stroked Hooker's neck, making him bob up and down. "This damn psycho chicken'll outlive us all."

I couldn't help but laugh because it was funny. The whole thing was funny. Well, the guy with the infected hand wasn't funny, and neither was the poor man who was still in with the doctor.

"Well, I'll leave you to it," I said to Truck. "Good luck."

I gave Maisie and Lizzy Taylor a friendly nod as I walked out, hearing Hooker screech a string of *fuck you, fuck you, fuck you*s as I left. I dashed back to my cabin to get away from the heat and the flies, and I couldn't help but wonder . . .

What the bloody hell had I got myself into?

Chapter Four

I STARTED MY REPORT, which was mostly introductory stuff, nothing major, and wrote notes about my conversation with the doctor.

I called my parents and told them all was well and reassured them, again, that I was fine. I wasn't being held hostage in some far-off foreign country because, god forbid, I leave Sydney's city limits.

My stomach reminded me to look at the time and I remembered Junie saying lunch was on in the hall between noon and one. Considering I had no other food other than the three pieces of fruit in my fridge, I decided to close up and head across to the hall.

And walked out into the baking heat.

It was so hot my shoes squished on the road like the rubber was melting. I had to squint so my eyes didn't dry out. My skin sizzled for the ten seconds it took me to walk there, the sweat searing like oil on my skin. It hurt my lungs, but oh boy, did it make me move.

I made it inside the hall, my hand to my heart, aghast. Humans were not supposed to live in this.

The hall, as it turned out, was full. Double the people from my welcoming party, which meant double the eyes on me. The ceiling fans were doing little to help combat the extra body heat in the room. My entrance earned me a few wry smiles.

Chappy took pity on me. He met me near the door and handed me a cup of ice-cold lemon water. "Looks like you could use this."

The drink was cold and wet, and I could have kissed him.

"It's hotter than hell out there," I said.

"Forty-seven today," he said. "Might wanna stay out of the sun."

Forty-seven degrees Celsius.

How was everyone not suffering heat-stroke? Even if they were used to this kind of heat, surely . . .

Chappy led me over to his table where Gibbo, JC, and Creepy were already eating. "Wanna get some grub? Still gotta eat, even when it's hot," Chappy said.

I looked at the smorgasbord of different foods. From what I could see, there was a heap of different salads and cold meats, pastas, curries and rice, a whole selection of fruit and bread. I wasn't expecting it to look so good, to be honest.

But more workers filed in, and they were all on a tight schedule. And they worked hard in the godforsaken heat. They needed it more than me.

"In a minute," I said. I was still too hot to think about food anyway.

Gibbo, JC, and Creepy thankfully left me in peace. They were talking about work—tonnage, payloads, and quotas. And I was grateful for the company without the conversation.

Then Bill came in with a stack of Styrofoam ice boxes on a trundle trolley. "Want me to put 'em straight in the cool room?" he called out to the kitchen staff.

Cookie waved at him from the stove. "Thanks, mate."

Wait . . . did he say cool room? As in a large, walk-in refrigerated room?

Refrigerated?

Leaving the mining conversation at the table, I followed Bill in through the back of the kitchen. "Need a hand with that?"

He shot me a smile. "Nah. Don't expect you to be helpin'." He opened the door and a rush of cold air hit me.

If outside was hellish, this had to be heaven.

Ignoring him, I took the top box off his stack. It was heavy as hell, but I walked it in. The cool room was about five metres square, with shelves of all kinds of food things. "Where do you want it?"

"Bottom left, under the shelf," he said, smiling. "You wouldn't be helping because of the cool room, no?"

I sagged. "I'm dying out there."

He just laughed and slung another heavy box in my direction. "You'll do yourself no favours by stayin' in here."

Admittedly, it was cold. Like two degrees, according to the temperature gauge on the wall. Nearly freezing, but I could deal with the cold.

"Just for a bit." I heaved the box down into the pile with the others and Bill brought in the next. "I could just stay for a bit, right?" There was an internal door handle and a light. I'd be fine.

Bill slid in the last box and stood up to his full height with a grin. "Well, I won't tell Cookie if you don't. But you should know not to piss off the cook."

I nodded and held up two fingers. "Two minutes."

So I sat my arse on a tall stack of boxes for two minutes and breathed in the cold air. I could feel my core temperature coming down already.

What a day. What a morning. The last twenty-four hours had been enough to make my head spin. I'd walked away from every single thing I'd known. Which was the plan, admittedly.

But now I'd done it, I had to wonder if it was the right thing to do. This little mining town was literally the most isolated in the country. In the middle of the desert, one of the hottest places on earth. And I came here in summer. What the hell had I been thinking?

I don't know how long I stayed in there. Longer than the two minutes I'd said I would, but still not long enough. Eventually, the cool room door cracked open, and I expected Bill's smiling face, or even Cookie's angry one . . . but nope. Dark blond hair, bright blue eyes, and a perfect smile poked his head in.

Davo.

"Thought I might find you here," he said.

"Oh." I straightened up. "H-hi . . ."

"Hang out in the cool room often?"

"Only when my internal organs decided that forty-seven degrees was a smidge too hot."

He walked in and closed the door behind him.

Oh.

Oh my.

He was wearing his work boots, a white singlet top, and . . . a pair of shorts. I was disappointed there was no skirt, but his legs were just as pretty as yesterday.

"Your pants and long-sleeve shirt," he said, nodding to my body. "Might wanna invest in some shorts and short sleeves."

I looked down at my trousers. "I actually don't have any work-appropriate shorts. I've only ever worn trousers to work."

Like every other person I worked with.

He nodded slowly. Then went with, "How was your first morning?"

"Well, I interviewed the doctor. Nice guy. Went into his waiting room to be met with a cat and a lizard. I've tried imagining the folks I'd meet out here, among other things, but a doctor that dabbled in veterinary sciences was not it."

He smiled. "Was it Maisie? And Lizzie Taylor?"

"Not sure I should divulge patient information."

He chuckled. "True."

"And then I was accosted and verbally assaulted by a cockatoo."

"Oh. You met Hooker?"

"I did. Lively fellow. Limited vocabulary, but he uses it in context, so that's nice. But yeah, that was how my morning's been."

Davo's smile was . . . oh boy, it was a freaking Colgate commercial. "Sounds like a Monday 'round these parts."

I sighed, not really having to say 'what the hell am I doing here?' out loud.

"It's so hot out there."

His smile faltered a little. "It is. But you shouldn't stay in here too long. It'll just make goin' back out there so much harder." Then he shrugged. "You're gonna need to get used to it. If you're sticking around, that is."

Did I really look that defeated?

Was I that defeated? I hadn't even been here a full day yet.

"Why did I have to pick the beginning of January to come here?" I asked, getting to my feet. "Middle of summer wasn't my finest decision. You know, in Sydney we can hit forty degrees. But it's humid. This is baking. Like an oven."

"It's not so bad." He opened the door and waited for me to follow him out. "You had lunch yet?"

"No, I thought I'd let the workers eat first."

He closed the door behind me. "Are you not here to work?"

"Well, I am, yes—"

"Then you should eat. Come with me."

I followed him out to find that most of the workers were gone and so was most of the food. Still, more than enough for me to pick at. I filled a plate with salad and cold meat, as did Davo, and then he sat at the table with me.

It was then that the heat began to creep back over me. No, not even over me. Into me.

Davo got up and came back with two cups of lemon water. "Drink up."

I felt so foolish. I should have known that going from hot to cold and hot again wouldn't be good for me. But I sipped the cool drink like a good boy. "I'm starting to think the cool room was not a good idea."

Davo smiled and swallowed his mouthful of salad. "It's tempting, and it probably helped a little initially, but it's better to try and regulate. You will get used to the heat."

This time he left the 'if you stick around' comment off.

"A cool wash towel or a bag of ice on the back of your neck," he added, "or on your chest will help. Or on the top of your head. Keep boiled water in your fridge at all times."

I knew all this, but for some reason, logic and common sense went out the window.

I ate some . . . then realised just how hungry I was and finished my plate in no time.

When I was done, Davo watched me take a decent

mouthful of water. "And if you wanna give me your pants," he said.

I almost choked on my drink.

He smiled wide and warm. "I can alter them for you," he added. "Into shorts. Or I could make you a pair from scratch if you'd prefer."

I collected myself enough to speak. "Oh."

"I'm handy with a sewing machine," he admitted.

That might have explained the skirt he wore yesterday. Or it might not. I was curious but didn't want to come right out and ask.

"That's good to know," I said instead. "I can't even sew a button on a shirt. I did bring some shorts, though they're just gym wear. Not very professional-looking."

"Do you think people around here would care?"

"Well, they're kinda short shorts. So maybe."

One of his eyebrows flicked upward ever so briefly, as if he wouldn't mind one bit.

"And my legs are so white that NASA needs to be notified before I wear shorts for possible light reflection so bright it can disrupt the International Space Station."

Davo laughed. "You're funny."

"It's a defence mechanism often found in nature in most redheaded mammals. Deflect the inbound insults so the predator loses the advantage."

His smile faded and he nodded slowly. "I see. An effective defensive tactic without using violence. As a male of my species who likes to wear skirts, I've found removing the teeth of a wannabe predator with my fist just as effective."

I met his gaze and nodded. *He mentioned the skirt . . .* "I can see how that would work. However, punching people in the mouth isn't a skill this pasty white redhead ever learned." I shrugged. "Personally, I was a very big fan of the skirt. Disappointed there wasn't one today, actually."

His gaze pierced mine and we sat there staring at each other. Not speaking, just staring. I couldn't have looked away even if I'd wanted to.

And I didn't want to. What I *wanted* to do to him was quite pornographic.

All of a sudden it was steaming hot again. Or maybe that was just me. I pulled at my collar. "Is it hotter in here all of a sudden?"

"Oh, yes." He smiled again, his blue eyes studying me far too intently. "I should go. I'll come and check on you this afternoon," he said. "See how you're feeling. Remember, cool washcloth, and stay hydrated."

I found myself smiling at him. "Yes, doctor."

AFTER I SAT in the hall smiling at where Davo had sat across from me, I remembered I had a job to do.

Instead of going back to my cabin, I went to the road-house in search of Junie and found her stocking the grocery section. "Afternoon," I said. "Busy?"

She smiled but kept stacking the packets of chips. "Always busy. Did you get yourself some lunch?"

"Yeah, it was great, thanks. It's so hot outside I'm pretty sure a portal to hell could open up out there and no one'd notice."

She smiled at that. "How're the people treating ya?"

"Oh great, thanks. Everyone's been nice so far."

She opened another box of Smith's Chips, but this time I helped her stack them. "How long have you been in Pannalego?" I asked.

"Since the mine opened ten years ago. Bill drove trucks through here, so he knew this petrol depot was here. We turned it into a proper roadhouse. We became the post office not long after we opened, and over the years the general store side of it just got bigger."

And then one of the workers came in. A woman Junie called Rachel, who had come in to collect a parcel. She bought a bottle of milk and a box of Frosty Flakes, thanked Junie, took her package, and left.

"It's amazing to me," I said, still unpacking packets of crisps, "how this community has adapted. What's essentially a truck refuelling depot has become a mail centre and a store. You're the hub of the town, really."

"Places like this are a dime a dozen in the outback. Just a necessity, really. Nothing special." Junie brought out a box of mixed toiletry items—toothpaste, condoms, Panadol, soap, and deodorant. Together, we restocked as needed.

"When was the last time you had a holiday?" I asked. "Time away, travel to some place different?"

She scoffed. "Had two days off once. Ate a questionable meat pie and spent one day in the bathroom, the next in bed. Does that count?"

I laughed. "Ah, no."

"No time for a day off anyway," she said. "What would we do if we weren't here?"

I got the feeling she never sat still. Ever.

Then Bill came in, wiping his hands on an old rag, grumbling as he went. "Busted radiator hose and lost the cufflink. Bandy ain't got none in stock either."

Junie frowned. "Bugger." Then she remembered . . . "Oh, Davo's going to Port soon. He'll be able to pick you up something."

I didn't understand what they were talking about, who

or what a Bandy was, or where the hell Port was or why Davo was going there. I could assume maybe it was Port Hedland? But it sure made Bill happier. "I'll go see him. Thanks, love."

Someone else came in, and Junie went behind the counter to serve them while I finished restocking. It was easy, and if it helped out, all the better. I wasn't paying them much attention, but when I'd finished, I caught the end of their conversation, talking about flight and shift changeovers for the FIFOs.

He bought a magazine, a bottle of Gatorade and some gum, thanked Junie, and went on his way.

"There's not much you don't know in the goings-on of this town, is there?" I asked.

"Nah. If someone wants to know something, they come find me or Bill."

Just then, Bill walked past the window outside. Junie shook her head as she went to the door. "Look at this stupid old fool." She opened the door and yelled at him. "Come inside before you drop."

Bill came in, and yeah, he was looking a bit rough.

She went to the freezer section and pulled out a bag of peas that had a big red tag with *not for sale* taped to it. She sat Bill down and shoved the frozen peas against his chest. "It's too hot out there for you to be walkin' down to Davo's. We have a telephone. Use it. You're too old to be out in this heat. You're not forty anymore."

Bill looked at me and rolled his eyes, but he patted Junie's hand and took the bag of peas, moving them to the top of his head.

"Want me to go get the doctor?" I asked.

"Nah, I'll be right."

Junie came back with a Gatorade and handed it to him.

"You can't be unloading the delivery truck, then working on the Cruiser outside in this heat, then go walking to the end of the lot. It'll cook yer brain."

He sipped it. "Thanks, love."

He looked better already but probably didn't want me hanging around. "Junie, is there anything you need me to do to help out?"

"Nah, but thanks anyway."

Someone else came in to be served and Junie went to help them. I gave Bill a pat on the shoulder. "Give me a yell if you need anything. Dunno what I'm good for but the offer stands."

He sipped his Gatorade. "Thanks, mate."

I left them to it and went back to my cabin. It was unimaginably hot, so I boiled some water and let it cool before putting it in the fridge. There was a small freezer compartment, so I made more ice, and I found a pedestal fan in the storage cupboard. I cleaned it up and stood in front of it and lifted the front of my shirt.

"No cool washcloths?"

I spun around to see Davo watching me through the glass door. "Oh, I . . . God, I . . ." I tucked my shirt back in, embarrassed.

He smiled as he let himself in. "It's the hottest part of the day right now," he said. "Why are you still wearing long pants? Did you do the wet washcloth thing?"

"I boiled some water and put it aside to cool before I can put it in the fridge. Not sure why I had to boil it, though. The tap water's scalding hot. Even out of the cold tap." Then I thought about what he said. "If it's the hottest part of the day, what are you doing out in it?"

He held my gaze. "I came to check on you, that you

weren't passed out on the floor or hiding again in the cool room."

I tried not to read anything into that. He wasn't here *for* me. He was just thoughtful and looking out for the new guy. In case I dropped dead from heat exposure.

"No hiding this time," I said.

"Take two washcloths, wet them thoroughly, fold them into quarters, and place them on a plate in the fridge. You can thank me later."

I smiled at him. "I can do that."

"Did you want to give me your pants?"

"Pardon?"

He smirked. "Your pants. I'll make them into shorts. Unless you wanted to wear the tiny gym shorts you mentioned."

"Oh." I let out a laugh. I'd forgotten about that. I looked down at my somewhat expensive trousers. "Hm, hang on." I found a less expensive pair and handed them over. "Do to them what you will."

"Hot pants with sequins coming right up."

"Uh."

He laughed. "Or a sensible inch above the knee?"

"I'm much more of a sensible inch above the knee kind of guy," I admitted. "However, I like shiny hotpants. Just not on me. Again with the blinding white legs. It's quite a look."

He grinned, and we stood there in my little cabin, staring, smiling. Until he took a backward step toward the door. "I better go." He held up the pants. "These won't take me long."

"No rush."

"There's supposed to be rain this arvo and a cool change coming tomorrow. You'll be fine."

"And by 'cool change' you mean it'll be forty-two degrees instead of forty-seven."

He smiled. "High thirties, at least," he said, sliding the screen door closed. "Dinner's at six. See you then."

My belly did an impromptu flip. "See you then."

CHAPTER FIVE

DAVO WAS right about the rain. It came over dark and humid, then began spitting welcome drops of water. I considered stepping out into it, dancing in it even, until the skies opened up and dropped a deluge of water.

I stood on my small porch and watched. The sound was deafening and the smell of it was amazing.

And as quick as it had come, it was gone.

But then the sun came out again and damn near boiled the puddles of water on the ground, but the air was cooler, and after a few minutes, it just all seemed . . . better.

Just like Davo had said.

Davo was something else. There was something about him I was having a hard time trying to get out of my head.

I told myself his dinner reminder didn't mean anything as I freshened up before dinner. It *didn't* mean anything. Davo was just a nice guy, and it had been far too long since I'd spent any amount of time with a *nice* guy.

I told myself it didn't mean anything as I used a little more deodorant in hopes of combating the inevitable sweat bomb that would hit me the second I stepped outside.

I told myself it didn't mean anything as I waited an extra five minutes so I didn't seem like I was counting down the minutes until six o'clock.

I didn't know Davo at all. Except that he had killer blue eyes, a heart-stopping smile, and incredible legs.

And that he was kind.

Honestly, kindness would win every single time.

Oh, and that he was wearing a skirt yesterday and not one person even blinked.

I told myself to stop being such a useless git and get my arse to the hall before he thought I wasn't coming or maybe that I was hiding in the cool room again.

I also told myself that he hadn't technically extended an offer for dinner, or any such thing, to me specifically. He just said dinner was at six and that he'd see me there. He was just reminding me of the time.

It absolutely was *not* a date, and there was a very good chance he'd be at a table with his mates and I wouldn't even speak to him. I prepared myself for that.

Until I walked in, and there were about a hundred people at tables, in the line for food, talking, laughing. So many faces, so much noise. It was loud and hot.

Jeez, it was very likely that I wouldn't even see him.

It was very likely I wouldn't even spot one familiar face, let alone his. That nauseating realisation hit me that I'd have to ask some complete strangers if I could sit at their table.

I was having flashbacks of my first week at college where I didn't know a soul, remembering how awful that had been, when I spied one familiar pair of very blue eyes smiling at me.

It made me giddy.

He was in the line-up, holding two plates, I just noticed, when he held one out as an invitation to me.

Now I could tell myself that didn't mean anything . . . but it meant something, right?

The way he smiled *meant* something.

"Thank you," I said, taking the plate. There was so much noise around us, so many voices, no one could have heard us. I was pretty sure no one paid us any attention at all.

"I was beginning to think you weren't coming."

"Traffic was terrible," I said lamely.

He'd waited for me.

He chuckled. "How was the rest of your afternoon?"

"Hot. How was yours?"

"Also hot. And busy. I finished your pants," he said. "Which are technically now shorts."

"Oh wow. You're very fast."

"It was easy. Took all of ten minutes."

"Well, I'm grateful. Thank you."

"Don't thank me yet. You haven't seen them."

"Are they hot pants with sequins?"

He chuckled. "I was tempted, but no. A respectable one inch above the knee, as requested." Then he leaned in a little closer. "You can always go shorter if you want."

A man walked past, somewhat resembling Ned Kelly. "Hey, Davo. What time you bunkin' out tomorra?"

"Six bells," he replied.

"Sweet."

We got to the front of the line and began filling our plates, and when we were done, we each filled a cup with lemon water, and Davo nodded toward a table.

There were other people at the table who all greeted us

with a "Hey, Davo" to him and a nod to me, and then they never looked at us again the whole time.

They were all very clearly used to eating and talking like this, in a cafeteria-style set-up with a hundred different conversations competing for volume. No one seemed to listen to anything they weren't involved in.

"So," Davo began after a few mouthfuls. "You're from Sydney, right?"

I nodded and swallowed my mouthful. "Born and bred."

"Long way from home."

"Yep. I wanted to get out of the city for a few weeks," I admitted. "Although my parents think I've deployed to Afghanistan or Rwanda or somewhere. I showed them on a map, but my dad kinda freaked out. He thinks anything outside a two-hour drive from Sydney is an epic journey. Like I'm leaving the Shire and heading to Mordor."

He smiled as he chewed. "Your dad didn't like the idea of you being on the opposite side of the country?"

I shrugged. "I think it was more that he didn't trust me to not get into some kind of trouble while being stuck in the middle of nowhere."

A smirk tugged at his lips. His eyes were dangerous. "Get into trouble often?"

This was definitely flirting territory. I had to make myself not smile. "Not at all. Though my dad and I would probably have varying degrees of opinion on that."

His eyebrow flicked upward as he stabbed some salad, and we ate in silence for a few bites.

"So, Fergus Galloway," he said as if he was trying my name out for size. "Your family Scottish?"

"My dad was born there. His family moved to Sydney when he was about six." I sipped my drink. "Doesn't have much of an accent anymore, but the love for the Rangers Football Club and Rod Stewart are firmly ingrained."

Davo smiled, licking his lips as he finished his dinner. "I thought Rod Stewart was English."

"Shh," I said in a panicked hush. "My father will hear. We don't talk about that out loud."

He laughed. "Funny."

"Oh yeah, sure, it's all fun and games until you have to eat salted porridge and have the police and fire brigade called to your house every Guy Fawkes night because your grandmother insists on lighting a bonfire in her backyard." That earned me one of his heart-stopping grins. "What about you? From where do ye hail?"

"Perth, originally. My family came from South Africa about five generations ago."

"Nice. And what do you do here? You're a permanent here, is that right?"

"Yep. I'm a hydraulic mechanical engineer by trade. Now I'm a leading supervisor."

"Interesting."

"Not really. It used to be fixing shit and getting my hands dirty. Now it's mostly writing reports."

I glanced at his oil-stained fingers. "Still manage some though."

He smirked. "When I can. We run a pretty big operation here and I'm *technically* a supervisor, but I'll use any excuse to help out on the ground. Maintenance and repairs are ongoing out here. Harsh conditions, and a mine that operates twenty-four hours a day."

"You didn't want to do the fly-in, fly-out thing?"

He shook his head. "Nah. I did in the beginning, but it just gets too hard. Not many can do it long-term. It was just easier for me to stay, and this place ain't so bad."

He talked about how they'd made their own community out here in the middle of nowhere. How sometimes on his days off, he'd drive the three hours to the coast and stay in Dampier or Port Hedland, but nowadays he didn't even do that much anymore. There was a town just over an hour away—an actual town and not a mining town—called Yillinali, and sometimes they'd go there and buy things they needed, but there wasn't much the internet, and the postal service couldn't deliver these days.

It dawned on me then that during the time I'd sat talking with him, I hadn't once thought about how hot it was. I also hadn't noticed that most of the people had cleared out and the staff had cleared away what was left of dinner.

I checked my watch. "Wow. It's after seven already."

Davo hesitated for a second, then stood up. "You up for a walk? I wanna show you something."

"Sure!"

I tried not to let my excitement get the best of me as I followed him outside. The sun was low and the air considerably cooler. And when I say cooler, I meant it was thirty-five degrees, but at least every beam of sunlight wasn't a burning laser.

But he walked, and I followed, quickly falling into step beside him. We walked along the roadway going past my place and walked in front of the neat row of cabins. Much like a caravan park, there were small roadways between rows. Each cabin of one of the permanent residents had something on their front porch to make it a home: flowerpots, wind chimes, bird feeders, or those spinning, colourful banners.

It was . . . nice.

"That's me there," Davo said, pointing to the last cabin

in the row. The one with the spinning banner. The rainbow spinning banner. But we didn't stop like I'd maybe hoped we would.

Would I go into his cabin with him if he'd asked? Did I want a quick physical encounter with him on my second day at camp?

If you say no, Fergus, you're a lying liar who lies. You know you would.

The rainbow banner had to mean what I thought it meant, right? We'd flirted a little and he definitely gave me the look a few times, but we'd skirted around any talk of sexuality.

I swallowed down my nerves. "Can I ask you something?"

"Sure."

"Yesterday . . . you wore a skirt."

He stopped walking. "And?"

Oh boy. "No reason," I said quickly. "I told you before I liked it. I'm not judging. Just wondered why you weren't wearing one today, that's all. I mean, the footy shorts are great and rather short, which I'm all for, to be honest. Maybe not quite as short as my gym shorts, which will probably be a good indicator as to why I won't wear them outside a gym. But if I can be completely honest, the skirt is prettier than the shorts. And your legs looked amazing. Not that I would ever try and tell anyone what they should wear. I was just curious, that's all."

He studied me for a long second, his defensive glare giving way to humour the longer I rambled. "I like to wear skirts. Always have. I like how they feel and how they make me feel." He shrugged. "Started back in high school. We did a swap uniforms day with the girls. They wore our footy gear, we wore their netball uniform. It was a pleated skirt and I just... I just loved it. And the reason I'm not wearing one today is because it's laundry day."

"Oh." I almost laughed. "Fair enough."

"Glad you liked it though. Not that I'd give one fuck if you didn't. I don't care what people think."

"Good."

He shrugged one shoulder. "There's been a few guys who took issue. Called me Priscilla, that kind of thing. One, that was a compliment. And two, they soon shut up when they realised I was their boss."

I smiled at that.

"And three," he went on, "I only had to belt the piss out of a few of them before they figured it was better to keep their stupid mouths shut."

I shouldn't have found that amusing—and I don't condone violence at all—but I'd be lying if I hadn't imagined my younger self shutting up a few of my school bullies like that.

"When you first walked in and I first saw you," I admitted, "I thought you were taking the piss out of me."

"What?"

Smiling, I nodded. "True story. I thought you'd all heard the new guy in town was a raging gay and you'd dressed up in a skirt to mock me. Or something. I wasn't exactly sure."

"Oh no," he said, shaking his head. "That wasn't . . . I didn't even know . . ."

I put a reassuring hand on his forearm. "It's okay. I figured that out when no one pointed and laughed at me. Actually, no one even looked twice at you wearing that. So I figured it happened a lot."

He sighed. "I'm sorry."

"Don't apologise. It was fine. Better than fine, actually,"

I admitted. "It made me realise that people might not care if they found out I was gay."

"No one's gonna care. The folks here are good people. From all walks of life, all a bit crazy, who all found somewhere to fit in." He smiled. "Come on, or we'll miss it."

"Miss what?"

He started up the embankment at the end of the camp. It was a levy of some kind, for water or noise, I wasn't sure. But when I got to the top . . . "Okay, wow."

The sunset. The sky was a palette of orange, pink, and purple. Cloudless, flawless. I'd heard about outback sunsets and seen a tonne of pictures, but none of them did it justice.

As far as I could see toward the horizon, red dirt was dotted with spikey grasses and an occasional pocket of pink and purple trumpet-shaped flowers—small, delicate, pretty. "What are the flowers?"

"Those are *Bonamia rosea*," Davo said. "Not many things bloom out here in summer, but they will after decent summer rain."

"How?" I asked. "How does anything live in direct sun at these temperatures?" I mean, surely, it was forty-seven degrees today.

"Some things thrive out here." He watched the sunset, the brilliant display of colour across the sky. "They adapt and find a way."

I got the impression he wasn't talking about the flowers, and I wondered what the purpose of this was. The conversation earlier about community, now showing me this, like he wanted me to see the beauty of this place.

"It is beautiful," I said. "Don't get sunsets like this back in Sydney."

"You probably do. Just too busy to stop and see it." He sighed and shot me a smile. "Life's a bit slower here."

Everything around us was aglow. The ground, the sky, the air in between us. Reds, oranges, pinks, purples.

I studied him for a long moment. How gorgeous he was. How he looked out across the landscape and the sunset as if it were the prettiest thing he'd ever seen. "Why did you want me to see this?"

He turned, his eyes cutting to mine. Soft, honest. "Because you're writing a report about us. You're from Sydney, and it scares me that you'll just think we're all country hicks in a backward town and that it's so hot out here, it's unliveable. When it's not like that at all. The people here aren't like that. Well, this town might be a little backward, I'll grant you that. We have some quirks. But anyone here would do anything to help you if you needed it."

"I don't think those things," I started, when the truth was, I'd thought all those things.

Davo glanced back toward the sunset, the changing colours washing over everything. "I wanted you to see that it can be beautiful here too, because from the look on your face this morning, I was sure you'd be packed and ready to leave already," he said quietly. "And . . ."

"And what?"

His eyes met mine. "And I'm away for three days and I'd be disappointed if you weren't still here when I get back."

Chapter Six

"When I walked into the hall and saw you," he said, "with your rusty coloured hair and freckles, well, I'd never seen a man so handsome. And then you shook my hand and you looked at me like maybe you wanted to get to know me a whole lot better, and I thought, wow, this guy . . ." He shook his head and stared out to the setting sun for a second. "Sounds crazy, I know, but I'd really like to get to know *you* better, Fergus."

I was so stunned by this upfront conversation, I almost forgotten to answer. *The way he said my name . . .*

"Y-yes. Sure. I'd like that too."

He grinned but then he made a face. "Do you have someone back in Sydney? Because I ain't the cheating kind. Even if you're just here for a while and they never had to know. That's not my style. Sorry, I should have asked first."

"No. There's no one. Well, there was," I admitted. "But he *was* the cheating kind. And also the kind to try and sabotage my career to better his own. So that ended all rather spectacularly a while ago. And now I'm here."

He gave me that killer smile. "I'm glad you're here."

And we did that stare thing, the is-this-where-we-kiss thing, but he looked away. "We should go . . . ," he murmured and nodded back down the embankment.

Was he implying we should go inside where it's private? Or . . .

We walked slowly and he eventually stopped out the front of his cabin. "This is me," he said again. He was nervous, chewing on his bottom lip.

Ask me if I want a drink.

Ask me if I want to go inside with you.

Ask me . . .

"Oh," he said. "Your shorts. Hang on one sec." He dashed up the two steps and into his cabin, re-emerging two seconds later with my shorts, neatly folded. "Here."

So I guess he's not inviting me in.

I took the shorts he handed to me. "Thank you so much. For doing this. You didn't have to."

"It was my pleasure. And I'd be lying if I said it wasn't an excuse to see you again."

Warmth ballooned in my belly. "You didn't need an excuse."

He looked at my lips, then back up to my eyes, let out a nervous laugh, and took a step backward. *He totally wanted to kiss me.* "So . . . JC's story time's about to start," he said. "On Channel five. He's just begun reading *The Hobbit*. It's really great. Everyone tunes in." He swallowed hard, shook his head, and took another step back. "So anyway, I'll let you go. I'll um . . . three days. I'll be back in three days."

Biting my lip, I managed to nod and walk away.

He wanted to kiss me. It was a buzz, a thrill of anticipation I hadn't felt in a long time.

Anyway, three days wasn't so long. It was just *three* days. There had been a cool change in the weather come through like Davo had said there would be, which meant the temps barely scraped forty degrees.

Which was still hot, but it wasn't atomic heat.

I interviewed a bunch of people—some permanents, some that chose the fly-in, fly-out life.

The consensus between the two was that the work was hard, the pay was phenomenal. What they didn't agree on, basically, was the FIFOs thought the camp was barely sufferable, while the permanents thought of it as home.

I was well aware that there were more factors at play than just attitude, but like the doctor had said, those who had decided to make Pannalego their home found it so much easier.

Those who chose to leave kept longing for home. They got sick of the shift work, of the long hours, of the heat, and the isolation. They got lonely. They missed their lives back home.

My focus had to be the human trials and tribulations, the hardships, the friendships. That's what I was here for. I wasn't here to get into the nitty-gritty of the mining industry. I was here to meet the people who worked in the environment and learn how they survived and thrived out here.

It was three days of interviewing some of the most remarkable people I'd ever met.

The food was good, and if it wasn't Junie or Bill keeping me company during mealtimes, it was Chappy, JC, or Creepy, or Truck and Bronnie.

It was almost as if Davo had asked them to keep an eye on me and make sure I didn't have time to hate the place because I was too busy laughing or listening to them tell stories.

I went to the bingo night. I listened to JC read from *The Hobbit* on channel five of the UH radio. He spoke so eloquently, he read so passionately, like a radio star or a book narrator, I was disappointed when he stopped at two chapters a night.

It helped pass the time, but it also helped me adjust to being here and to get a better understanding of the good folks that lived here. Not that there was much else to do at night time. The whole camp was quiet, lights out by nine o'clock, because they were all up before the sun the next morning for a twelve-hour shift in the mine. Or they did night shift. Either way, nights at Pannalego were dead silent.

I spent my nights on my bed, under the ceiling fan, letting my mind run wild. Thinking about what Davo had said to me as we watched the sunset.

How he'd wanted to kiss me. The way he'd looked at my lips.

He wanted me to be here when he got back.

He had to do a three-day health and safety course in Port Hedland, and this happened about every three or four months. All the supervisors did it. No big deal.

He just wished he didn't have to go now that I'd arrived.

And damn if that should-we-kiss buzz kept me on a high for three days. And I didn't know exactly what time he'd be back to camp on day three, but I woke up excited.

Which was utterly stupid.

I wrote more of my report, I did some laundry. And I'd had myself convinced Davo wouldn't be back until the day shift ended after six o'clock, but dinnertime came and went and there was no sign of him.

By seven-thirty, I decided to head to Junie's store in the roadhouse for a bottle of Sprite for a sugar fix before JC's reading on the radio at eight.

The sun was getting low as I went past the hall and

headed toward the roadhouse, the sunset just as pretty as usual. There was one ute refuelling, which I didn't pay much attention to, and another that was coming into camp. I didn't look twice at it either until it hooked a U-turn and pulled up right by me.

I was startled and was just about to give them a rightful lecture on road safety when the man got out.

He wore the bright-orange hi-vis clothes all the miners wore, boots, and he was covered head to foot in red dirt. His hair, his face, clothes, boots, covered in dirt and grime.

But then he smiled that goddamned Colgate smile, and I recognised who it was.

"Howdy," Davo said, still grinning.

"You scared me," I said.

"Sorry."

"I'm not an expert in body language but I'm almost certain that smiling like that negates the apology."

He laughed. "I'm glad you're still here."

My heart thumped so hard it almost hurt. "Yeah, some nice guy showed me that it could be pretty for five minutes every day, while the other twenty-three hours and fifty-five minutes are blisteringly hot."

His smile became a grin. "Nice guy, huh?"

"Well, he was. Until he just almost hit me with his ute."

"Were you heading inside?" He quickly ran to open the roadhouse door for me. "Nice guys also open doors, see?"

I stepped inside, smiling as I slipped past him. "Thank you."

"Ah, Davo," Junie called from the other end of the store. "Got a parcel for you. Arrived yesterday. Just grab it for ya."

I went to the soft drink fridge and took out a Sprite, and he was right behind me when I turned around. "So," he said quietly. "I was wondering . . . if you'd like to come past my place. In about an hour? I need to shower and . . ." He held out his dirty, grimy hands. "Scrub myself. If you're not busy. And only if you want to, that is."

My gaze darted from his lips to his eyes, back to his lips.

He groaned softly. "God, I should have kissed you the other night," he murmured.

"I'll just throw it in your ute," Junie said, carrying a rather large box outside.

We watched her, then Davo turned back to me. "If you don't want—"

"Oh, I want."

His grin was immediate. "Give me half an hour."

"I thought you said an hour."

"I was trying not to sound desperate."

I laughed and he backed away, turning just as Junie came back in. "Popped it on the passenger seat for ya, Davo."

"Thanks, Junie."

"Here, you missed dinner. Take a sandwich. And a banana."

She shoved a small bag into his hands. "Thanks, Junie. You're an angel."

"Good to have you back, love."

He slipped out the door and I was left standing there holding a bottle of Sprite, smiling like an idiot.

"You okay there, Fergus?" Junie asked with a sly smile. "Look like the wind rattled your sails."

My brain kicked into gear. "Oh, sure. I'm fine." I put the bottle on the counter. "Just this, please."

She scanned it and I tapped my card at the EFTPOS machine.

Junie held the bottle hostage. "You know," she hedged. "Davo's one of the good ones."

Oh my.

Was she . . . ?

Was this a shakedown?

"And I know you're new here, and you won't be here for long," she went on. "But we all love him to pieces."

Oh my god. This *was* a shakedown.

"And we'd just hate to see him get hurt." Junie frowned. "So if you weren't aware, he's been looking in your direction, if you know what I mean. And if you're not inclined, perhaps it'd be best to let the good man down gently."

Horrified didn't begin to cover this.

"Oh." My mouth was as dry as the dirt outside. It made my voice crack. "Yes, well. Perhaps I *am* aware, and perhaps I *am* inclined. If you know what I mean."

Junie sagged with relief and smiled. She put her hand to her chest. "Oh, thank the heavens. Because I've never seen him smile at anyone the way he was smiling at you just now."

Oh, wow. Okay.

What was I supposed to say to that?

Junie beamed like a proud mum. "I put condoms in the bag with his sandwich. Just so you know."

"Oh my god!"

"No need to be embarrassed."

"I'm not embarrassed. I'm mortified. Why would you assume we'd need those?"

"Because I was young once, and the roadhouse closes at eight. Did you want to get caught out?"

"Well . . . no, but—"

"So don't keep him waiting." She winked. Actually winked.

I wanted to die.

"Can I . . . have the Sprite, please?"

She looked at it in her hand as if totally surprised to see she was holding it. She thrust it at me. "Yes. Of course."

I backed out of the store and hurried to my cabin. So much had just happened. Davo was back and disappointed he hadn't kissed me the other night. He'd wanted to. I'd wanted to. Hell, if we weren't in the middle of the road-house, I would have. And Junie gave me the riot act and I just came right out to her.

Literally.

Told her I was . . . inclined.

I should have told her it was none of her business, but I didn't think that was true in this town. Everything was everyone's business here.

And this wasn't even getting into the whole condom conversation, which I was, absolutely one hundred per cent, going to pretend never happened.

Most importantly, I had twenty minutes before I was going to Davo's.

Where we would be alone, presumably. *He wanted to kiss me.* The way he stared at my mouth . . .

I was going to kiss him back.

And he had a box of condoms.

Christ.

No. For our first *encounter,* kissing would be enough. It would be sweet and new. Exciting and *enough.*

I told myself that as I walked down to his cabin, thankful it was dark. No pressure, no rushing, no games. We were grown men, adults, knowing full well what we were doing.

And this wasn't a booty call. Maybe he just wanted to talk, I reasoned as I knocked on his door.

"Come in," he said. "It's not locked."

I opened the door and stepped inside. His cabin was

much like mine: a sofa and TV on one side, a small dining table and kitchenette on the other. Though on his table sat a sewing machine and bunches of different fabrics.

I didn't have much time to look any closer because Davo stood between the bathroom and bedroom doors, rubbing a towel over his hair. "I just got out of the shower," he said. "No amount of scrubbing gets that dirt out. Sorry I was a bit late getting back to camp. I came back from Port Hedland and there was an issue with a truck at work and . . ." His words trailed off with a smile.

I couldn't stop staring. He was almost naked except for a purple, shiny skirt. Mid-thigh, loose and flowy, and it did absolutely nothing to hide the bulge in his crotch.

He was ripped, tanned. Muscular shoulders, a splash of hair on his chest, flat stomach, defined thighs. And a purple, shiny skirt.

"It's satin," he said softly. "You like it?"

I tried to lick my lips. I could barely nod. He was the most beautiful juxtaposition I'd ever seen.

"Fucking hell," I breathed.

He threw the towel into the bathroom and smiled at me. He ran his hand down over his thigh. "Wanna feel it?"

I managed a nod this time, and he took the two steps it took to stand right in front of me. I could feel his body heat, fresh out of the shower. He smelled of soap and men's deodorant. It was intoxicating.

He took my hand and my heart banged around like a pinball in my chest. He placed my palm on his hip, his hand over mine, and slid it down his thigh.

I didn't dare breathe.

The satin was as soft as it looked. It felt like silk. It was cool; his skin was hot. I thought he might let my hand go, but he threaded our fingers on his thigh and together we lifted the satin up. Slowly, inch by inch, up the outside of his thigh.

My lungs squeezed and I remembered I needed air.

He smiled as I sucked back a ragged breath. His eyes were dark and beckoning. "You like it?" he murmured.

"Hm." My brain was fried. I'd never been so turned on. "Yes."

He grinned. His tongue poked out the corner of his mouth. I put my other hand on his side, his waist, feeling the taut muscles under my palm.

Then I made the mistake of looking down. The bulge in the front of his skirt was now caught in the bunch of the fabric, and satin was unforgiving.

It spared no detail.

It was glorious.

"Davo," I said, my voice a gruff whisper.

"Kiss me," he begged.

I pulled him flush against me, hard, crushing my mouth to his. I drew my hands up to hold his face, kissing him with every ounce of passion and desire in me.

Open lips, tangled tongues, imploring, demanding. And he let me. Leaning into me, giving me his mouth to do with as I pleased. His hands wound around my waist, pulling me closer. His erection pressed against me, mine against him, and I kissed him until we both needed to breathe.

He kept our hips pressed together, but he leaned back. His lips were wet and kiss-swollen, his eyes heavy-lidded. He had *fuck me* written all over his face.

"I told myself kissing you would be enough tonight," I breathed.

"But?"

"But I want to do so much more." I tried to kiss him again, but he pulled away, a sultry smirk on his lips. And keeping our hips joined, he stepped backwards, walking me into his room until his legs hit his bed.

So with one arm around him, I lowered him onto the mattress and kissed him as I sank my weight on him. His legs widened, our hard erections rubbing together, and I gripped his hip.

Satin, smooth, soft.

Sexy.

He rocked his hips, moaning, whining, and holding me so tight like he needed me closer, like he couldn't get enough.

I couldn't get enough.

Shit.

I was so turned on. He was going to finish me just like this. "I'm going to come," I rasped.

I ground against him and he arched his back, digging his fingers into my skin, and his cock pulsed against me as he came first.

Holy fuck.

Watching him orgasm, feeling it, holding him as tremors of pleasure wracked through him, pushed me over the edge.

I came so hard.

Wave after wave surged through me and I cried out with the force of it. When the room stopped spinning, Davo was cupping my face, tracing his thumb along my jaw. "Holy shit," he mumbled. "That was so hot."

I barked out a laugh, still lightheaded, and fell onto the mattress beside him. He wiggled over, resting his head on my arm. "I had every intention of showing restraint," I said. "And I was hoping for maybe just a kiss."

Davo laughed, leaned up on his elbow, and kissed me. "You can kiss me any time. The way you kissed me by the door? That was filthy hot."

"I was going to say it was the skirt, but honestly, I'm pretty sure it was the whole package. Freshly showered, shirtless, your body."

"And the skirt."

"Well, yeah. The bulge in the skirt sealed the deal."

He hummed happily. "You really liked it."

"Oh yeah. And to be completely honest with you, I've never seen a man in a skirt before. Never even thought about it, actually. Until I saw you."

He pulled at his skirt, or more accurately, at the wetness. "And I just washed it."

I chuckled. "I need to get cleaned up too."

"I noticed you were wearing the shorts I cut off for you."

"They're great, thanks."

He rolled off the bed. "I'll grab a wet washcloth."

We cleaned up the best we could, and I sat on the sofa to wait for him to change his clothes. He came out still shirtless but wearing a different skirt. Mid-thigh, cotton. "No sexy satin again?" I joked.

He did a bit of a twirl before he sat at the end of the couch, one leg folded underneath him, facing me. He tucked his skirt down to cover himself. "This is an old comfy favourite. Hope you don't mind."

"Why would I mind? It's cute as hell."

He gave me a sweet smile. "Thank you." Then, like he just remembered, he leaned over and turned the UH radio on. "It's almost over." And sure enough, JC was reading another chapter of *The Hobbit* on-air. We only caught the last five minutes or so.

"He has a voice for radio," I said when it was over.

"Doesn't he? It's magical. And it's not just everyone at the camp that listens. Truckies tune in all up and down the highway. The mine's aerial is huge, so they can listen."

He poured us both a drink of Diet Coke and handed me a cup, and then I remembered . . . "Oh, did you have your sandwich?"

"Yep."

"Junie told me what she put in the bag," I admitted. "I almost died of embarrassment. She just came out and said it."

Davo grinned. "I laughed when I saw. I'll have to thank her tomorrow." He was quiet for a few long seconds. "Sooo, about using those . . ."

My eyes went to his. Considering what we'd just done, I guessed it wasn't too early for the sex talk. "Yes? Any requests in mind?"

He laughed, blushed a little. "Could *often* be considered a request?"

"I believe so."

"And *thoroughly*."

I ignored the way my dick was beginning to enjoy this. "Also a qualifier, I believe."

"What about *deep*? It's been so long since I've had a good pounding."

Holy hell.

I had to palm my dick, and he laughed when I gave him a gentle shove. "Jesus, you can't say shit like that to me. Or I'll be fulfilling all requests tonight."

He grinned, his tongue playing with his top lip, his eyes full of mischief and desire. He leaned back and ran his hand down his belly, lower, and lower . . . "All of them?"

Chapter Seven

Davo was face down on his bed, arse raised up high, fists clutching his pillow. He whined at me to hurry the fuck up. He was pushy, desperate. Bratty.

I hadn't planned to be fucking him tonight. But as I knelt behind him, stretching and lubing him, I'd never wanted anything more.

I rubbed the head of my cock over his hole, and he pushed back, desperate. He wanted it so bad. I slipped my thumb inside him again and he straight up growled at me. "Fergus, stop fucking teasing me."

So I gripped his hip, angled his arse just right, and pushed my cock into him. Hard. Hard enough to pin him to the mattress. His back arched, his eyes and mouth open in shock. I held him down with my body, whispering gruffly in his ear. "Is this what you wanted?"

I slid all the way in, balls deep, and he could only whine in response.

I dug a little deeper, pushing his arse up as I drove into him. "Answer me, Davo. This what you wanted?"

He stretched his arms above his head, still fisting the pillow, and drew his arse up. "Yes. God yes."

He was hot and tight, and I was glad we'd brought each other to orgasm earlier or this would have lasted all of ten seconds.

But I gave him what he asked for. Thorough and deep as I pounded into him. I ran my hands over his back, his shoulders, gripped his hips, and drilled him. I kissed his shoulder. I whispered in his ear words that made him groan.

"You're so hot."

"You're so tight."

"You feel so good."

"You like it deep?"

"You're gonna make me come."

And he met every thrust with a moan for more. Every murmur in his ear earned me a grunt of satisfaction. The harder I fucked him, the faster he jerked himself . . . until he began to tremble, and he cried out when he came.

I drove into him as deep as I could. His arse milked me, his orgasm igniting my own, and I filled the condom deep inside him.

We collapsed onto the bed, sweating, panting, the room and the world around us spinning.

"Holy fuck," he mumbled.

I began to slowly pull out, to get my weight off him, but he quickly grabbed my arm. "Stay there."

If only I could.

I never wanted to leave the warmth, the pull of his body. But I had to. Keeping my chest to his back, I pulled my dick out of him and rolled us onto our sides, making him the little spoon.

"You feel okay?" I asked, trailing warm kisses across his shoulder. "I was pretty rough."

He stretched and wriggled a little bit, then he laughed. "I feel amazing." He sighed happily, sleepily. "You did everything right."

I kissed the back of his head. "So did you."

A blissed-out silence settled over us, and I could have so easily fallen asleep. Davo was almost out to it, so content in my arms.

I didn't want to leave, but . . . "I should go," I murmured.

"Nuh-uh," he protested sleepily.

I almost felt bad. I'd worn him out and he had to start work at six in the morning, after getting up at god only knew what time this morning. "Stay in bed," I murmured before extracting myself. I pulled the sheet over him before kissing the side of his head. "Night."

I woke up much later than I'd anticipated, and with a persistent hard-on. Like not having sex for a few months and then having two rounds of the best orgasms ever had woken my dick up.

I lay in bed atop of the sheets, half-awake, remembering Davo the night before. His strong, masculine body under me, how he begged me for it, how he took it.

His skirt.

I really didn't curse too often, but holy fucking hell.

I gave myself a few long strokes at the memory. How he tasted, how it felt to slide inside him, that tight warmth, the way he moaned. The way he came while I was buried inside him.

I fisted my cock harder, my balls heavy and tight. I imagined my hand was his body, taking me again and again.

I shot hard, ropes of come spilling over my fingers and onto my belly.

My head was full of a sultry smirk, blue eyes, and wet pink lips.

I refused to believe I was in trouble.

This was just a short-term fling. I was only here for four weeks. Four weeks to write a full report that both the government and the mining industry would likely just ignore. Four weeks to have some laughs, meet some great people, have mind-blowing sex, then go back to my real life.

I wasn't in trouble.

Showered and dressed, I needed to do some laundry because my shorts were still a little crusty from last night. While I waited for the washing machine, and because I'd missed breakfast, I went to the roadhouse.

Of course, Junie was behind the counter. "Oh, good afternoon," she said. "Sleep late?"

It wasn't afternoon. It was just after nine in the morning.

"I did happen to sleep late, yes," I admitted.

"Same reason Davo was smiling this morning?"

I fought a grin. "I have no idea what you're talking about."

She raised a brow. "Hm, that's what I thought."

I tried to play it cool and straightened the gum on the counter. "Just out of curiosity, how smiley was he this morning?"

Junie laughed and picked up a grey box of mail. She slung it onto the counter and began sorting it. "I don't wanna know details. Like hearing about your own kids having sex. Would rather not know. As long as he's happy, I'm happy." Then she added, "And safe. As long as he's being responsible."

Oh god. Here we go again. But while she was on the topic, now was as good a time as any . . .

"Oh, speaking of which," I said, taking a packet of condoms from the hygiene section. "Might need more of these."

And then, of course, Bill happened to walk in. "Oh, thought Davo looked a bit happier this mornin'."

I looked at Junie, horrified. "Oh god. Does everyone know?"

She shrugged. "Probably not everyone. Give it till lunchtime today."

Oh, for Pete's sake. "Nothing's secret in this town, is it?"

She shook her head slowly. "Nope."

Bill was still caught up in his side of the conversation. "He dropped off the gear for the Cruiser this mornin' on his way to work. Grinning from ear to ear, he was. Even Gibbo noticed."

"Well, if Gibbo knows, you won't need to wait till lunchtime." Junie checked her watch. "Everyone will know by now."

I sighed. "Excellent."

Bill nodded. "Yep. We've got a tele-gram, a tele-phone, and a tell-a-Gibbo. If you want someone to know something . . ."

Awesome.

"So," I said. "Anyway, I have some online meetings today. Thought I better get something to eat before they start." I headed over to the grocery section and grabbed a box of cornflakes, then grabbed a bottle of milk and went back to the counter. "Anyway, I better be getting back, but if you need a spare pair of hands this afternoon, I'll be free after two. Just unpacking boxes or restocking shelves. I'd be no good to you helping outside because . . . well, because

I'm a city boy with a complexion to match this." I held up the milk. "But the offer's there."

"Aren't you doing more of yer interviews?" Junie asked as she rang up my items.

I added some gum to my purchases. "I can do those any time. But I learn more about the people and what goes on around here by being part of it, not just asking questions."

The idea of them needing me for anything was ludicrous. After all, they'd run this place like a well-oiled machine for a decade.

I paid and took my bag. "No big deal either way. If you think of anything that needs doing, let me know."

I took my breakfast back to my cabin, then hung my laundry out. It'd be dry in fifteen minutes in this stupid heat, but it got me thinking, or wondering, why I'd offered to help out at the roadhouse or why I'd spend my entire afternoon there if they'd asked.

And from an anthropological viewpoint, or even a psychological one, I could chalk it up to simply wanting to help or the need to be productive. But I knew, analytically and compartmentally, though I wouldn't admit it to anyone, it was probably closer to wanting to be part of the community.

I wanted to be included. I wanted to contribute. It didn't exactly make sense, but I wanted to . . . I wanted to be a part of something. Even if it was just for a few weeks.

I wanted to belong.

I ate my cornflakes and refused to think about what any of it meant.

I sat through my first online meeting that, despite dragging on for far too long, honestly should have been an email with half a paragraph and maybe three bullet points, max.

But the big boss liked to see faces, no matter where we were in the country or around the world.

Did that make me feel included? A part of something?

Nope.

It wasn't the same.

The second meeting was with our department manager, Michael. It was more personal, with fewer faces and more open dialogue. I was more comfortable with this group, especially now since my least favourite asshole was no longer on the team.

My closest work friend, Nisa, smiled at me on-screen, and a few seconds later, my phone buzzed with a message. *FaceTime after? Have news.*

I replied. *Sure.*

The meeting went around to each of us, and we briefly described any ups or downs we may have had.

"Fergus," Michael said. "How is the remotest town in the country?"

"It's hot." I laughed. "No, it's actually great. Very small, close-knit. It's basically a caravan park for two hundred shift workers. The water is hotter from the cold tap, and everything is covered in red dust. They hold bingo nights. Some guy reads a book over the local radio twice a week. I think tonight is karaoke, which I will not be attending. Oh, and there's a cockatoo that swears like a sailor."

That earned me a few smiles.

"The locals treating you okay?"

My mind immediately went to Davo and exactly how he treated me last night. "Yep. Very welcoming."

No sooner had the meeting ended, my FaceTime chimed. I answered and Nisa's smiling face filled the screen.

"Want to explain exactly how the locals have been 'very welcoming'? Because the smile, Fergus, gave you away."

I laughed. "No."

"Didn't think you would."

"What's the goss?" I said, sipping my water. "Give me all the details."

"Well, it's not great," she said. "You know how the Melbourne Uni research team had their funding cut?"

We ran a sister squad with the Melbourne team. Instead of competing for prestige, we often collabed on findings to broaden our knowledge pool. They'd recently had some government funding cuts and we wondered when the axe would swing in our direction.

"Yeah, sure. Have they confirmed anything for us?"

Nisa shook her head. "Not yet. But I heard something very interesting." She leaned in toward the screen. "Guess who was allocated extra funding?"

My stomach sank and I sighed. "Canberra."

She nodded.

The Canberra team, like us, was supposed to be separate from government bias. That was how research worked. However, Canberra was the political capital of Australia. The Canberra University was a feeder school for political science students.

The fact that they were now allocated a greater percentage of funding reeked of bias.

"Goddammit."

She nodded again. "That's what I said."

Pretty sure her response would have matched Hooker the cockatoos. But anyway . . .

"The department heads are having a meeting later this week and they were told to expect changes. Michael didn't want to say anything in the online meeting until he knows more, but I think we can assume the cuts are coming."

Fuuuuuck.

Nisa nodded. "Yeah."

"I thought you meant news as in gossip, like Tim from downstairs got caught in the photocopy room with Leslie."

Nisa laughed. "That's a mental image I'll need lobotomised, thanks."

"You're welcome."

"Sure you don't want to spill the deets on that smile, Ferg?"

"Nope."

"Haven't seen you smile like that in a long while. Must be the outback air agreeing with you."

"Yeah, the air. Let's go with that."

Her smile softened. "It's good to see your stupid face."

I laughed. "Good to see your stupid face too."

"I better go," she said. "Oh, and I have to say absolutely not one person misses your fuckwit ex."

I burst out laughing and she ended the FaceTime with a grin.

I was getting way ahead of myself on whatever it was Davo and I had going on. Waaaay ahead.

I was beginning to think I might be in a small spot of trouble.

I WAS RIDICULOUSLY EXCITED to see Davo at dinner. His shift ended at six, which meant by the time he showered and came up to the hall, it'd be about half past.

I'd almost forgotten about Junie telling me everyone in the camp would know about Davo and me . . . until I walked in. This time when most eyes fell on me, they were accompanied with a knowing smile.

Just great.

And then I'd had a terrible thought that maybe after what he'd got from me last night, he wouldn't be interested in seeing me again.

We hadn't exactly talked about expectations. Hell, we hadn't even talked about seeing each other again once, let alone regularly. Sure, he'd said *often* was a preference, but that didn't mean anything.

And here I was kinda assuming we were what? Dating?

I was an idiot.

And sure, Junie had said Davo was smiling this morning, but that didn't mean anything. He was very likely smiling because he got some the night before.

He wasn't smiling because of me.

I was a bloody idiot. And I didn't exactly want to be laughed at in front of a hundred or so people who were watching me, waiting for Davo to rock up so everyone could have a good laugh.

I grabbed a plate and filled it, despite the sudden loss of appetite, and found a quiet table.

I'd pushed my salad around with the fork so much it was beginning to wilt. The salad, not the fork. And my mood. I tossed my fork onto the plate, about to get up and leave, when a familiar pair of legs stood by the table, wearing work boots and a red skirt.

"This seat taken?"

I looked up at his face and my ridiculous heart skidded in my chest. I grinned. "Hey."

So much trouble.

Davo put his dinner on the table and sat opposite me. "You looked like someone kicked your puppy."

"I was . . ."

Did I mention he was wearing a singlet top? An oversized surfer kind—so old it had holes in it—and his blue eyes were assessing me so hard I lost my train of thought.

"Oh, I was waiting for this guy to finish work. He's kinda great. Anyway, then I had this sinking feeling that he maybe didn't want me to wait for him to have dinner. We hadn't discussed any such things, and I had this horrifying thought that maybe he might have just used me for a night, if you know what I mean. And he was going to walk in, and it was going to be some kind of joke, and everyone would laugh."

He was staring at me, his fork stopped halfway to his mouth. He put it down. "There was a lot in that we should probably unpack, but first, maybe we should talk about why you're so sure I'm going to prank you and people are going to laugh at you."

"Oh, um . . ."

"Is that what your ex did to you?"

I met his concerned eyes. "Yes."

"I'm not him."

"I know. Sorry. It's a reflection on me, not you."

He ate a few bites. "You should eat something. You'll need the sustenance for later."

I couldn't help it. I laughed. "You're confident."

"Well, what you did to me last night," he whispered. "I was hoping that was an encore."

I groaned out a laugh. "I would have no problem with that."

He ate some more, clearly hungry. "And just so you know, I want you to wait for me to have dinner. And I didn't use you for anything last night. I experienced it *with* you, if you'll remember."

I nodded, my heart squeezing. "Oh, I remember."

"And I know we never talked about . . . well, anything. So we should do that first. How long are you here for?"

"Another three weeks."

He made a face and sighed. "Well, for those three weeks, you can assume you have a date for dinner and plans for every night that will probably involve a lot more of what we did last night."

Holy hell.

"If you want," he added.

"I want."

He smiled. "Good." He ate some more and finally managed a smile. "So, now we cleared all that up, how was your day?"

I chuckled. "It was pretty good. I had some online work meetings that I had to sit through. I was hoping to catch up with Creepy after lunch. I wanted to ask him some questions, maybe see that artwork of his you mentioned. But he wasn't in."

"Nah. On his days off, he goes out with the doc in the afternoons. Doc searches for gold. Creepy looks for anything left behind by old miners or campers. Stuff he can use in his sculptures."

"Oh, yes. The good doctor showed me his metal detector."

Davo's smile widened. "He's got gold fever. Spends all his spare time out in the desert, has for ten years. He won't come home one day, and we'll find him at the bottom of an old mineshaft. Or snakebit. But Creepy's a good guy."

"Can I ask why you call him Creepy? He doesn't look creepy. He's been super nice to me every time I've spoken to him."

Davo chuckled. "Nah. His first name is Tim. He gets called Creepy because his surname is Crawley."

I laughed. "Creepy crawly. That's kinda funny."

"Everyone here has a nickname of some kind." He ate a section of orange. "Well, except me. I'm just Davo. First name David."

"You don't look like a David. You look like a Davo."

"I'm surprised no one ever called me Klinger. You know, from *M*A*S*H*?" He shrugged. "Kinda disappointed, to be honest."

"I can start calling you that if you want."

He peeled another section of orange and smirked. "No, I'm good, thanks."

I tried not to sit there smiling at him like a fool. "So, while we're talking about names," I said. "Can I ask about the cockatoo? I hear it screeching bad language every so often. Why is its name Hooker?"

I regretted asking as soon as the words were out of my mouth.

"Because it's seen a cock-or-two."

I sighed. Totally should have seen that coming. "What about Truck? Because he's a diesel mechanic?"

"Nope. Truck's real name is Laurie."

Oh dear.

"You know, as in lorry."

"Yeah, I got it, thanks."

"And JC is short for Jesus Christ."

"Because of his long hair?"

"Nah. Because he put a metal spike through his hand. Crucifix style."

I had to swallow back a laugh. "Right."

"His left, actually. His real name is Ian."

"That's funny."

He finished his drink and sighed. "Have you had enough to eat? You didn't eat much."

"Yeah, I'm fine, thanks."

"Wanna get out of here?"

I nodded and we walked down to his cabin, but if I'd assumed he was going to pounce on me as soon as we were through the door, I was wrong. He led me to the couch and he sat, taking my hand and giving me his undivided attention.

"Now, tell me about this arsehole ex-boyfriend of yours."

Oh. Okay. I wasn't expecting that.

"He cheated on me. With the HR manager at work. I'd applied for a promotion to run my own team, and as it turned out, so had he."

"Holy shit."

I nodded. "Yep. We met at uni, ended up living together, first just as flatmates. Anyway, he decided he'd better his chances in his big promotion plan by offering his arse to the HR manager while telling them that I was a slacker and how all the other staff hated working with me, blah, blah, blah. Anyway, I didn't get the promotion. But neither did he, which was funny, at least. Anyway, I gave notice on our rental because it was all in my name, and when he finally manned up enough to come home, begging like the dog he was, I told him he had less than forty-eight hours to have all his shit out and find somewhere else to live."

Davo laughed. "Good."

"But my new apartment is small and kinda terrible, and this job came up. They needed someone with feet on the ground over here, and I wanted to get as far away from Sydney as I could."

"Well, you did that."

I sighed. "He was an arsehole. He often made me the punchline of his jokes to make his friends laugh. You know, nothing outright horrible or mean, but enough to chip away at me. In the end, I expected it."

"Enough to make you think I was pranking you to make everyone look and laugh at you."

I made a face. "Sorry. I know that's not you."

He squeezed my hand. "I'm sorry he did that, and I'm sorry you didn't get the promotion."

"I wouldn't be here if I got it."

"Then I'm not sorry."

"Neither am I. I'm glad I'm here."

He smiled at me, his eyes soft. "So," he murmured. "Ask me about my day."

"How was your day?"

"Funny you should ask," he said, smirking. "I spent all day thinking about you. About what you did to me last night, about the ache in my arse, about what I want you to do to me tonight."

From sweet to scorching hot in half a second.

"Hope you weren't operating any heavy machinery while you were thinking about me."

He grinned. "I was, actually. I had to check the lubrication system on an engine. You know, where the pistons drill into the cylinders over and over, in and out and in and out, and so yeah, I thought of you."

I laughed. "I'm really not familiar with the mechanics of engines."

He bent his leg, spreading his knees, pushing his skirt down to cover his crotch, but he kept his hand there. "Lucky I do. Is there anything you want to ask me?"

"Only a couple hundred questions."

His tongue poked out the corner of his mouth and he grinned when my eyes tracked its teasing journey. "First question?"

I looked him over, from his spread legs, his hand over his crotch, the red fucking skirt, the singlet top, and his knowing grin. My gaze finally drew up to his eyes, finding fire and invitation staring back at me. "How bad's the ache in your arse?"

His grin widened, then his legs.

Yeah. I was in so much trouble.

CHAPTER EIGHT

I woke up in my bed just after six in the morning. It was hot already, but I didn't seem too bothered by it. I smiled at the ceiling, my mind replaying last night. How we'd made out on his couch, how I took him to his bed, how I worshipped his body, kissing and massaging his back as I sunk into him, giving him exactly what he'd wanted.

Over and over.

I groaned at the memory, ignoring how my body reacted.

How could I possibly want more?

I'd had more sex in the last few days than I'd had in months. And the best sex I'd probably ever had. Davo was so receptive, so attentive, so perfect.

He sure was something special.

I'd left him sated and sleeping, with a kiss to his temple, and fell into my own bed for one of the best night's sleep I'd ever had.

I was already looking forward to tonight. I had a dinner date, apparently. For tonight and every night I was here, and basically all the sex we could have.

Davo wanted it. A lot of it, all the time.

He didn't get the opportunity often, I guessed, and he wanted as much as his body could take while he could get it.

I was more than happy to give it to him.

My dick perked up at the thought of more sex with him. I ignored it and rolled out of bed.

Showered and dressed, I began my day. I made it to breakfast before they cleared it all away. I wanted to catch Cookie before he got too busy.

I had a bunch of questions about how he found the supply chain, how he stayed inspired to feed two hundred people three times a day, every day of the year.

He didn't seem too impressed with the interruption.

"It's fascinating to me," I began, figuring flattery would help, "that this community thrives in the face of adversity. The heat, the isolation, the hardships. There are few things that keep the wheels turning out here, and you're one of them. Junie and Bill at the roadhouse too—don't get me wrong—but if you were to walk out and never come back, this whole place would grind to a stop."

He put the bag of potatoes on the stainless-steel benchtop and turned his dark stare at me. "What are you greasing my chain for?"

"What?"

"If you want something specially made, add it to the list." He pointed his chin toward a clipboard hanging on the wall by the door. "And I'm telling ya right now, if it's that fancy city shit, you can forget about it."

I wasn't sure what constituted 'fancy city shit' but that was beside the point.

"No, no. I don't want to add or request anything. I'm stoked with what's on offer. I didn't know what to expect, but I'm very impressed."

He studied me some more, almost squinting as if he was trying to see through the lie.

I shrugged, aiming for indifference. "I just wanted to ask you how you do it? How many staff you have, menu planning, ordering, and deliveries. How it all varies from where you've worked elsewhere. That kind of thing."

He stared some more and made an unhappy sound. I was pretty sure his grumpy demeanour was normal and not directed at me personally. I thought he was going to tell me to sod off, but instead, he pursed his lips and glared at me. "Can you peel potatoes?"

Shit. "Well, yes. Probably not as fast or as well as you'd prefer, but yes. I can peel potatoes."

"You peeled potatoes?" Davo asked me. We were sitting at dinner, eating, talking, and I was telling him about my day.

"Yes. Potatoes first, then carrots, and I started to cut the pumpkin, but he took the knife off me and told me to wash up instead. Well, it involved some cursing, but I'm sure you get what I mean."

Davo laughed. "Sounds about right."

"So I had to do manual labour for my conversation with him. Which I didn't mind, actually. It was fun. And honestly, I was so bad at it, no one has to worry about him asking me to help out again."

He grinned as he chewed and swallowed. "Did you get the information you were after?"

"Yep. He's very proficient. And I hate to use a cliché, especially to the mechanically minded, but he runs his entire operation like a well-oiled machine."

"He does."

"And between him and Junie and Bill, they've got this whole place well-supplied and organised."

Davo nodded, though from the set of his eyes, I got the impression he didn't entirely agree with me.

He put his fork down. "So, how's the report coming along?"

I took a deep breath. "Good. Any report we do needs to be submitted in a particular format. I'm still gathering information at this point, making notes."

"About what?"

"The people. The characters I've met. The conditions, adversities, and triumphs."

His gaze met mine, a smile played at his lips. "And what will you say about me?"

I laughed. "Oh, believe me, that's not making print."

His smile widened. "Shame."

"I don't think my boss would appreciate the play-by-play account as much as I would."

He chuckled and sipped his drink, but his smile faded away. "It's not all adversity out here."

"No," I agreed. "There are triumphs."

"But you assume those triumphs correlate to the adversities." He met my gaze, challenging, engaging.

"Do you not consider the isolation and extreme heat an adversity?"

He seemed to consider this for a second. "No. It's just what we do. We just get on with it. No point in complaining."

That made me smile. "That's the attitude I find so impressive."

"What, a general optimistic attitude?"

I chuckled. "Well, yes."

Davo smiled at me. "The folks that fly in, fly out might tell you a different story. But the few of us that live here, live here because we choose to . . . this is our home, and we like it. Living here is not a prison sentence."

"Anthropologically speaking, I find it fascinating that some people thrive in extreme climate conditions. Humans have inhabited deserts like the Simpson or the Sahara for tens of thousands of years. And the subarctic circle. How they regulate and maintain sustainable body temperatures is an adaptation in survival, even evolution. As is how they obtain their food sources."

"We have refrigerated trucks that bring food," he said with a hint of sarcasm. "It's not like the early settlement days where camel trains had to trek for weeks."

"No. Modern technology allows for the adaptation of humans to survive almost anywhere. Not to mention the science and medical advancements that make living in harsh environments easier. Life out here is fine while there's access to essentials like food, shelter, and fuel. But if they become difficult to source, then humans have to adapt and, in all likelihood, move."

"Like nomadic tribes' people."

"In certain cultures, yes."

His eyes narrowed, his expression guarded. "Or when a mine closes and the mining community is left without resources to sustain life."

I closed my mouth. I didn't want this conversation to turn sour; I was just enjoying having an actual conversation with him.

He smiled again, but it wasn't exactly happy. "Have you considered why all the cabins here are removable, trans-portable?"

I winced. "I had, yes. I'd like to think cost was a factor.

And having each cabin off the ground allows for air circulation and cooling."

His smile became a smirk. "That's a very optimistic attitude you have there."

I found myself smiling back. "Thanks. I grew it myself."

He laughed, his eyes softening. "Living out here might be crazy to you, but the idea of living in a city where it's overcrowded, with rush hours, traffic jams, and no open space . . . Well, that's crazy to me."

"That's just city life though. Not really extreme climate conditions."

"True. But there are pros and cons for living anywhere." He held me with his gaze. "Like in Sydney. You can probably get any kind of food you want at any hour."

I nodded. "Sure."

"But you've never seen the stars above the outback desert at midnight. Or the desert wildflowers bloom in winter."

His words thumped in my chest, right alongside my heart.

I shook my head. "No, I haven't."

"It's so much better than any food you can get at 3:00am. You need to feed the soul too."

I was smiling at him again. "But that's just it. It's my whole point. You find beauty in the world around you. My first day here, I thought I was going to die, and you were like, 'But look how pretty the sunset is, isn't it worth it?' and that's an extraordinary perspective. Folks here value community and people over material possessions, and honestly, that's refreshingly human."

He chuckled. "Thanks. I think?"

"Oh, believe me, it's a compliment." I was still smiling at him. I wasn't sure if I'd stopped yet. "And you might think that choosing to live here is *just what we do* and *we just get on with it*, but I can tell you, those of you that choose to live and thrive where the outside temperature can kill you are remarkable."

"We're not remarkable." He shook his head and shrugged. "We're just . . ."

I leaned in, ensuring his eyes met mine. "You're remarkable."

His smile was sweet, even a little shy. "You're not *too* unremarkable yourself."

God, the way he was looking at me.

It was suddenly hotter in here, and that had nothing to do with the temperature outside. I looked around at the now-near empty dining hall. "Oh. Everyone's gone."

He drew his bottom lip between his teeth, his gaze burning into mine. "Should we go?"

I gave a nod. "Can you think of anything you'd rather be doing right now?"

He laughed. "Why, yes I can. How about you?"

"Hmm." I pretended to have to think about it. I checked my watch. "I have about four and a half hours to wait until I can see the outback stars at midnight."

"Are you teasing me?"

"Yes."

"Just as well." He shook his head. "Anyway, there's a better place to see the stars from."

"Where?"

"Werrimirrah Gorge."

"And where's that?"

"About an hour and a half drive." He chewed on his bottom lip again. "I have four days off three days from now. We could camp out there one or two nights if you want?"

"I want."

He grinned. "Speaking of want . . ."

"Yeah, let's go."

On the walk to his cabin, I really wanted to hold his hand. My palm itched to grab his, entwine our fingers, but I cursed internally at myself for wanting foolish things.

Handholding. Jeesh, Fergus. That's not what this is.

He unlocked his door and stood aside for me to enter. I was suddenly nervous, with no reason as to why. We'd done all kinds of things in bed. I'd seen the most private parts of him.

But there was a tiny seed in my chest that yearned for something more.

Something deeper.

The way any seed yearned for sunlight and water, I wanted to grow something with him.

Physical touch, kissing, handholding. I wanted romance with him.

God.

It sure explained the nervousness.

Davo went to the fridge, and I stood there, wanting to make conversation before we fell into bed.

"Is this your latest creation?" I asked, nodding to the fabric on the table.

He cracked the lid on a bottle of water, took a sip, and handed it to me. "Ah, yeah. I've barely started it. It's kinda silly."

Silly?

"It looks like a lot of fabric," I said. I didn't know the first thing about sewing or material. "Why is it silly?"

He shrugged but went to the sewing machine and held up a piece of fabric. "It's tulle. Like for a tutu?" He smiled awkwardly. "I ordered the material. Remember the box that Junie put on my front seat the other day?"

I nodded. "When you got back from your three days away."

"I haven't really had time to make it. Been kinda busy every night." He waved at me. "Believe me, I'm not complaining."

I chuckled. "But why is it silly?"

He inhaled deeply and let it out with a sigh. "I just wanted to try it. You know, a tutu kinda skirt. They're . . . uh. I dunno."

"They're what?"

His gaze met mine. "They're pretty."

I don't know why that felt like such an admission, but it made my chest feel all warm. "They are very pretty."

His gaze went to mine, and he stared before that shy smile tugged at his lips. "It's not going to be an actual tutu," he said, his cheeks a little pink. "More of a flared skirt with a lot of tulle. I won't wear it out in public."

"Why not?"

"It's, uh . . ." He sighed. "I dunno. It's different. Just for me."

I held his gaze. "Then it's not silly."

He smiled, looking down, his cheeks a flush pink. I held out my hand, and after an unsure second, he took it. I sat on a dining chair and pulled him onto my lap. He was considerably taller than me this way, so I had to stretch up to kiss him.

"If anything makes you feel good about yourself, then it's not silly," I murmured.

He cupped my face and planted a soft kiss on my lips before resting his forehead on mine. "Thank you."

"If you wanted to work on the skirt, I don't mind."

He frowned. "It can wait."

"You sure?"

He nodded. "Yeah. I'd rather spend my time with you."

I traced my fingers down the side of his face, from his eyebrow down to his jaw, and swiped my thumb along his bottom lip. It felt way more intimate than I'd intended. "You can do both," I said. "I'm happy to sit and read or watch something on TV while you do your thing."

His eyebrows knitted and his frown deepened. "I'd rather not waste a minute with you. The skirt will still be there in three weeks."

But I wouldn't be.

Wow.

I hadn't expected that to hurt like it did.

"Ouch."

He tried to smile but it went wrong. "Yeah." He stood up, but only so he could straddle me. He had to hitch up his skirt and he laughed. "Ooh, another bonus."

I gripped his hips, the skirt all bunched up, and pulled him closer to my groin. He lifted his legs and rocked, grinding on me. Leaning down, he forced my head back and kissed me, all open mouths, teeth, tongue.

He drew a groan out of my throat, and it spurred him on. He ground down on me harder, wanting, desperate.

I broke the kiss. "Should we give your arse some reprieve tonight?"

He shook his head, then stood up and took my hand, leading me to his bedroom. "Absolutely not."

CHAPTER NINE

THE NEXT DAY, I finally caught up with Creepy and he showed me the art he'd made over the years. They were sculptures, using recycled materials, mostly metal but not always.

There was a goanna piece a metre long. I could make out horseshoes, old food cans, banged out and flattened but still recognisable. Aluminium cans for the underbelly for contrast, bike chains for a tail. It was incredibly lifelike.

An emu that stood over five feet tall. Each 'feather' was pressed metal over the body, which looked to be a motorbike engine casing.

A kangaroo that appeared to be entirely made out of old car parts. It had hubcaps for leg muscles, a grill for the pouch, red brake-light casings on its chest, and various engine parts I couldn't recognise.

There was an echidna, a wombat, and a wedge-tailed eagle in full flight. Bolts, nuts, springs, cogs, spanners, metal piping, aluminium, steel.

"Oh my god," I whispered. "These are amazing."

He gave a single nod. "They take some time."

"Do you sell these?"

"Nah."

"You should."

"Wouldn't know how," he said. "Or how to transport them. They're heavy buggers."

"I could help you."

He side-eyed me. "Why?"

"Because you should sell these. Or display them, at least. Is there a gallery in Port Hedland or Dampier?"

Creepy laughed really loudly. "Kid. You're funny."

I sighed. "Well, a website is easy to set up."

He shook his head. "Nice to dream, but no. Besides, you might not wanna look too close. About ninety-nine per cent of what I use is junk I've found. Like old farm machinery, abandoned car parts. Things get left in the desert all the time, and the heat and sand make them unusable pretty fast."

"And the other one per cent?"

"Well, just between you and me, if the local government roads and traffic department have any old signs go missing, I wouldn't know anything about that."

I laughed. "No one has to know."

He pinched the beak of a brolga statue, as though he was so familiar with it, like he knew every plane of metal by feel.

"So," he said nervously. "You and Davo, huh?"

Oh my god.

"Yeah. I guess?" I really wasn't sure why he was asking or where this conversation was going.

"He's . . . he's a good guy."

Oh, for crying out loud. This was another shakedown.

"Yes, he is," I replied. "If you're going to put the 'hurt

him and they'll never find your body' speech on me, you're too late. Junie's beaten you to it."

He chuckled. "Well, I dunno about never finding your body."

I couldn't even be mad. "I know he's a good guy. I know he's one of the sweetest men I've ever met. He's smart and kind and funny. He works hard. People respect him. I get it."

Creepy relaxed then. "I remember the first day I ever met him. First day at work. I'd come from another mine up north. I'm a fabricator by trade, right? I weld stuff. We'd had the drive shaft of a truck clear snap. It must have been fifty degrees that day, and I had to weld underneath the truck. He stayed with me. Covered from head to foot in red dust, so hot it almost killed us, but he wouldn't let me do it alone."

"That sounds like him."

"Then later that night, he walked into the dinner hall wearing one of his skirts. I didn't recognise him." He shrugged. "Not because of the outfit, but because he wasn't covered in red dust and grease. But then he smiled."

I chuckled and nodded. "Sounds familiar."

"Sat himself down right in front of me and we talked about work, and I didn't once think about what he was wearing. No one does."

"I noticed that," I admitted. "On my first day. No one looked twice."

"I just didn't want you thinking any less of him. Some-one's clothes don't make them any less—"

"No!" I put my hand to my chest. "Oh no, no. Person-ally, I'm a huge fan of the skirts. Like, huge fan. If you get what I mean."

It took a few seconds before he cottoned on. "Oh."

I laughed off my embarrassment. "And I would never

judge anyone for what they wear. I believe in the freedom of expressing yourself. Like your artwork. It's an extension of who you are. And if I'm being honest, that's my most favourite thing about this little town. Everyone's free to be themselves. No one bats an eyelid."

"It's a great little town we've got here."

"It really is."

We both stood there, nodding, for a bit too long, and it appeared our conversation was over, so I said, "Thanks for speaking to me today. I do appreciate it." I began to leave and stopped, adding, "If you want to sell these sculptures, just let me know. I'll help any way I can."

He waved me off, but as I walked up the road, he called out, "Don't forget it's international food night tonight."

I smiled and waved, though I had to wonder what horrors of cultural appropriation I was going to walk into.

Luckily Davo called out as I was walking over to the dining hall. "Hey, wait up," he said, jogging a little to catch up. Tonight he wore a black tank top with a black pleated skirt that went down to his knees. It looked a bit kilt-like, and I was not opposed.

"Wow."

He grinned. "You like?"

"I love."

He gave my hand a quick squeeze before letting go. "It's a bit heavier. I don't wear it in summer too often."

"That's a travesty. You should wear that all the time."

He waggled his eyebrows. "Even in bed?"

"Yep. Or over the table. Over the end of the couch. Maybe up against the kitchen counter? I could lift it and be inside you so easy."

He stopped walking, let his head fall back, and groaned. "You can't be saying shit like that to me." Then he hissed, "I cannot be getting a hard-on in a skirt. There's no hiding that."

I laughed. "Sorry."

He gave me that perfect grin. "Come on, I'm starving. Been hanging out for this all day."

We began up the ramp to the dining hall, and this time, I stopped. "What exactly is international food night? I have visions of corny, borderline racist paraphernalia, and I'm not sure I can condone that. I'd rather eat my cereal back in my cabin than take part in that."

He laughed and dragged me inside. The dining room was packed, loud, and happy—clearly a very popular night. And then I saw why.

Instead of trays of different cuts of meats, veggies, and salads as there had been every night, now there were trays of different noodles, dumplings, grilled and spiced fish, different rice dishes, meat on skewers, eggs, and broths.

"Oh my god. There's sushi."

Davo handed me a plate. "What do you want first?"

"All of it."

He laughed, but I wasn't kidding. I put almost one of everything onto my plate, and he smiled as he watched me eat. "You like it?"

I spoke with my mouth full. "It's so good."

He grinned. "And you wanted cereal?"

I swallowed my mouthful of dumpling. "I had visions of . . . well, I wasn't even sure. Good intentions but sorely misguided appropriations. That's what I envisioned." I cringed. "Maybe someone dressed up like Papa Giuseppe handing out garlic breadsticks, doing terrible Michael Corleone impersonations with a drawn-on moustache."

Davo laughed really loud. "No!"

"It's not funny. When I was in college, I went with a

friend of mine back to her hometown a few hours out of Sydney. It was a backward place, and they meant well, I guess, but they had an international food night at the local pub, and I swear to baby Jesus, it was so horrifyingly bad. Picture every possible racist stereotype, and you can begin to understand why I had reservations about eating dinner tonight."

Davo was still laughing. "Were there really *The Godfather* impersonations?"

I shook my head sadly. "Don't even get me started on the French guy."

Smiling, he ate some rice with egg and pointed at it while he chewed and swallowed it. "Every two weeks we have this. Where we are right now, we're closer to Indonesia and Singapore than we are to Sydney or Melbourne."

"Good point."

"Most of Cookie's staff are from all parts of Asia. He takes the night off and they do everything."

I looked around, then leaned in to whisper. "They're better at this than him."

Davo chuckled, his mouth full. "Don't repeat that."

I waved my hand. "No, of course not."

He smiled at me for a bit, but we ate in companionable silence. "So, I was thinking," I began.

"Oh? Is this a good thinking or a bad thinking?"

I chuckled. "Well, good. I hope."

He waited for me to continue.

I took a deep breath. It's now or never. "So I was thinking you should make the skirt. The tulle one. The one you've wanted to make for a long time."

He studied me for a long moment. "Why?"

"Because you've wanted to do it for ages, right? And I don't want you to not be you just because I'm here."

"Are you saying you don't want to come back to my place anymore?"

"What? No!" I shook my head quickly. "No, jeez. I still want that. A lot, actually. Like all the time."

He smiled. "Then what are you saying?"

"That we can do both? Like, if you wanted to work on your sewing, I could just hang out at your place, or not, if you'd prefer I didn't." I shrugged. "I just want you to . . ." I groaned because this was all coming out wrong. "Okay, so I want us to hang out. Watch TV, cuddle on the couch. I don't want to *just* have sex. I want to do other things with you as well."

Smiling, he gestured to our plates. "Like dinner every night?"

I rolled my eyes. "Yeah, okay. Sorry." I immediately felt foolish for saying all this stupid shit out loud. My stomach suddenly wasn't feeling too great. "Forget it."

He reached across the table and took my hand. "I was joking."

"Hey, Davo," a guy interrupted us. I'd seen him around but didn't know his name. He was the guy who looked like Ned Kelly.

"Hey, Ned."

I withheld the sigh—or the laugh—that tried to escape.

Ned was holding a work shirt. One of those bright-orange, hi-vis kind, though this had a whopping rip. "Ahh, well ya see, m'shirt got into a fight with a star picket," Ned said. "Was hoping you might be able to perform a miracle? I've only got two."

"Yeah, no worries. Leave it with me. I can fix it tonight."

"Aww thanks, mate." Then Ned gave me a nod. "Sorry to interrupt."

He left us and I was trying to avoid Davo's piercing gaze, considering how we'd left our conversation.

"That was Ned," he said.

"Let me guess. Ned because of Ned Kelly?"

"Nah, not in the beginning. He used to just have a mo. The real bushy kind. So he was Ned Flanders, but then he grew the beard. Then he became Ned Kelly."

I tried not to smile but failed. "Of course."

Davo waited for me to look at him. "Wanna go?"

I nodded, and as we walked out of the dining hall, I went down the ramp and headed toward my place.

"Hey," he called out. He pointed his thumb toward his cabin. "Thought you wanted to hang out?"

"Yes, well," I began, watching his smile get wider and wider. "Are you joking again?"

He laughed. "No. I'm fine with hanging out. But you did specify that we could do both, right? You said hanging out *and* banging, yeah?"

I rolled my eyes and walked over to him. "Oh, a smartarse, I see? If you want both, I'll give you both, and I won't be gentle with either."

He laughed. "Don't tease me."

"Shut up."

"So tell me, how does one 'hang out' gently?"

I put my arm around his shoulder and whispered as we walked, "First, I have you on your knees on the bed, face down, arse up so I can hitch your skirt up, and plough into you."

He almost tripped over his own feet. "That's not . . . God, I told you I can't get a hard-on when I wear a skirt." He held Ned's shirt down to hide any bulges. "And anyway, I'm pretty sure that's the banging part, not the hanging out part."

We got to his cabin and I followed him inside. "So," I said, taking Ned's shirt from him. "What did you want to do first?"

He glanced at his bedroom door and his fingers played with the hem of his skirt. "Umm."

Jesus.

I grabbed his arm and led him to his bed. "Get on your knees."

I lifted his skirt up and pulled his briefs down.

I told him I wouldn't be gentle.

I wasn't.

CHAPTER TEN

AFTER BREAKFAST, there was a knock on my door. Had anyone apart from Davo visited me in my cabin? I didn't think so.

I opened the sliding door to find Truck giving me a very desperate smile. Hooker perched on his arm. He was holding a lunch box in his free hand. "Morning," Truck said. "I normally wouldn't ask—"

Hooker spread his wings out. "What the fuck do you want? What the fuck do you want? What the fuck do you want?"

"—but I was just called into work. Bronnie's on the six o'clock shift and we can't leave his asshole at home by himself."

"Fuck you, fuck you, fuck you, fuck you."

"You want me to look after him?"

"Just for a couple of hours," Truck said. "Normally Chappy can take him, but he's on night shift."

"What the fuck do you want?"

Truck turned to the giant bird. "You behave yourself. I told you to be nice."

"Fuck you, fuck you, fuck you, fuck you." Hooker bounced up and down, his crest up. He was enjoying this.

"Oh, I have a work meeting this morning," I tried.

"I wouldn't ask if I wasn't desperate," Truck said, coming inside. "It's too hot to leave him outside. He can't stay in his cage all day, and last time we left him alone, he chewed up the couch. Like the *whole* couch."

I looked at the bird. He bounced up and down. "Fuck you, fuck you, fuck you."

Truck shoved the lunch box in my hand. "His food. He has a feed mix and some fruit and stuff. And he'll need cooled boiled water."

"Uhhhh."

He put Hooker on the back of one of the dining chairs like a perch and gave me a grimace-smile. "Thank you, thank you," he said, backing out of my cabin. He pointed his finger at Hooker. "You be good, so help me."

And he was gone.

And it was just me and Hooker.

I looked at the giant fucking bird in my very small cabin. "Well—"

"What the fuck do you want? What the fuck do you want?"

"Manners!" I yelled at him.

Hooker blinked, then did that bouncy dance he did. "Fuck you, fuck you, fuck you, fuck you."

I sighed. "Okay, look. We're gonna have ourselves a little English lesson. You and me. Starting now."

"Fuck you, fuck you—"

I held up my finger. "No. No, fuck you. No. I won't tolerate that language."

Hooker was quiet for about five seconds. He stared at me with his beady little black eyes.

I waited until he was calm and tried for our first lesson. "Say hello. Hello, hello, hello, hello, hello."

Hooker bounced up and down, spread his wings out, and let out an almighty screech. It sounded like I was murdering him.

And then he let rip. "Fuck you, fuck you, fuck you, fuck you."

I gave him my sternest look and held up my finger. "No. Stop that. You will not speak to me that way."

He squawked some more, then proceeded to screech at the top of his huge bird lungs.

"Stop that now!" I yelled at him. "Or I will put you in the fridge."

He stopped.

Oh my god.

That actually worked.

I would never actually put him in the fridge, and I had no idea where those words even came from. But it worked.

"Good boy," I said quietly. "Quiet boys don't go in the fridge."

I sounded like Hannibal freaking Lecter.

But he was quiet for a solid sixty seconds. He began to bounce up and down again on the back of the dining chair, so I poured him some water and gave him some of his sunflower seeds.

Which he tore into and left the casings all over the chair, table, and floor.

"No, please," I said. "Go right ahead. I'll clean up after you."

He held another seed in his little grey claw and looked me dead in the eye as he ripped into it, ate the seed, and spat the casing onto the floor.

"Thanks."

"Fuck you."

"You have a terrible attitude."

"Fuck you, fuck you, fuck you."

"Do you want to go into the fridge?" I pointed to the fridge. "Wanna have a nap in there?"

"No, no, no, no, no, no, no, no, no, no."

"I didn't think so."

"What the fuck do you want?"

"Manners! I want some manners. And a little appreciation here. I'm trying my best—" I stopped. "I'm talking to a bird. Oh my god, I've lost my mind. I'm talking to a bird."

I checked my watch. I had five minutes before my meeting started. "Shit."

"Shit, shit, shit, shit, shit, shit."

"Oh, you can learn that."

He squawked at me and did his bouncy dance.

"I have an important meeting," I said, ignoring his little preen at my expense, and opened my laptop. "I'm gonna need you to be on your very best behaviour."

I considered putting him in the bedroom until I remembered that Truck said Hooker had destroyed their couch. Then I considered the bathroom. There wasn't much he could destroy, but he could hurt himself.

I snatched up the apple and cut it into slices. He was very happy with this development, bouncing and whistling as he watched.

"You like apple?" I asked. "Good boy. Quiet boys are good boys. Quiet boys get apple."

And now I sounded like a creepy sex offender.

This was all so wrong.

"Just please be quiet," I said, handing him his first piece of apple.

He was quiet while he ate. This was good.

I opened my laptop, and he was still quiet. Well, he made a happy, bouncy song as he ate his apple. And I hated to admit that he was kinda cute.

Then he jumped onto the table, clearly wanting more apple. He jabbered away to himself as he did his little waddle, then he began to bounce again. "Fuck, fuck, fuck, fuck."

I held up a finger. "No. No swearing. Be a good boy."

I logged into my work Zoom before giving him more apple. I had to space out the snack distribution, try to buy myself some quiet time. The screen began to fill up with squares of my colleagues. Nisa gave me an indiscrete wave.

And Hooker was happy with his apple while the meeting started and everyone got settled . . . until Michael, my department boss, spoke. Then Hooker bouncy hopped over to me, curious, cute. And evil.

I handed him some apple and whispered, "Be quiet."

"Fergus?" Michael asked. "Something to share?"

"Oh no," I said quickly. "Sorry. I'm just babysitting at the moment."

"You're babysitting?" he asked, his tone flat. Nine faces all stared at me. "Did you just tell a child to be quiet?"

Wait, what? "Oh no, it's not a human child. It's a forty-year-old sulphur-crested cockatoo that has an attitude problem and a vocabulary that consists of only swear words."

I turned my laptop so they could see Hooker. He wasn't exactly hard to miss. He was a bright white bird the size of a cat sitting on my table. He lifted his little foot and bit into some apple, and he bounced and mumbled his little song as he ate.

So cute. So deceiving.

Everyone oohed and aahed. "Don't be fooled," I said, turning the screen back to me. "He's evil."

Michael was smiling. Everyone was.

But then Hooker bounced right over to me, until he was in full view of everyone, and tilted his little evil head at the screen. "Fuck you, fuck you, fuck you."

"No!" I said, giving him some more apple. "I told you no swearing!"

"No, no, no, no, no, no. Fuck, fuck, fuck, fuck."

Nisa was laughing. So was Toby, the guy from the financial division. Lindy, the snooty, pretentious one, was horrified, her hand over her mouth.

Michael was no longer smiling.

"Sorry," I said. "He got dumped on me twenty minutes ago. It's too hot for him to go outside. It's like forty-five degrees here today. Apparently, he spent the first forty years of his life with Wally, a guy that swore a lot. As you can tell. The result being a bird that's more like a senile grandpa who screams at everyone to get off his lawn, all while having the attention span of a toddler."

Hooker poked his head in front of the screen from the side. "What the fuck do you want? What the fuck—"

"Hooker, stop it." I gave him more apple.

He didn't want it. He wanted to stare at the screen, bounce up and down, and scream obscenities.

Nisa was laughing so hard she was crying, Toby doubled over laughing, and even the old guy from resources was now smiling.

Michael wasn't.

I had to speak over the squawking. "I'll put myself on mute. I'm sorry."

I hit mute and turned up the volume so at least I could

hear what was going on. I pulled over the lunch box and took out some celery, which Hooker threw on the ground.

I spied the broom in the corner, so I rested one end on the table and the other on the small kitchen countertop, making him a perch.

That kept him happy for most of the meeting, thankfully. He bounced on it, waddled on it, sharpened his beak, and swore a lot. He came over and peered at the computer screen a couple of times, bouncing and cussing some more. Thank god I'd muted my screen.

"Okay, before we get to the gritty part," Michael said. "Fergus, can you hear me?"

I gave him a wave and a thumbs-up.

"Good," he said. He took a deep breath. "So as you know, budget cuts are always something we contend with. We've dodged the last few, however, I don't think any of us will be surprised to learn our funding has come under some scrutiny this time. They're making some significant cuts."

My stomach sank.

"What kind of cuts?" I asked, then realised he couldn't hear me. I hit unmute and asked the question again. I wasn't the only one.

Michael seemed to hold his breath. "About half."

"Half? Half of what?" Nisa and I asked at the same time.

Hooker decided to pipe up with "Fuck, fuck, fuck, fuck, fuck, fuck" while doing his little bouncy dance, and I was going to reprimand him, but honestly, same, bird. Same.

Other people asked questions, all at the same time. Michael put his hand up to stop the chatter. "I wish I had more information for you at this point in time, but I don't. I think we can expect redundancies, replacement contracts." He shrugged. "I don't know who. Could even be me."

My phone beeped with a message from Nisa.

WTF? We knew it was coming but OMG

Michael sighed. "Anyone on field duty right now can expect a phone call from me after this meeting. We'll have to look at cutting all trips short and getting you home. You might want to wrap up any ongoing appointments you might have."

No, no. Wait . . . I wasn't ready to leave.

"What?" I asked.

This word, of course, was all the permission Hooker needed. "What the fuck? What the fuck? What the fuck?"

I shrugged without a hint of apology. I pointed my thumb at Hooker. "What he said."

My humour fell a little flat, given everyone was now grim-faced. They were cutting our team in half. When we'd heard rumblings of budget cuts, I expected purse strings to be tightened. I hadn't expected to be fired.

I hadn't expected to have my trip cut short. I hadn't expected to meet Davo. I certainly hadn't expected to leave him so soon.

The meeting ended with Michael promising to be in touch. Most of the screens logged off, so I did the same.

Nisa sent me another message. *Call me as soon as you speak to him.*

I closed my laptop and Hooker decided to make it his dancefloor, which was fine. My mind was swimming, my heart feeling all kinds of heavy.

I didn't want to leave Davo just yet.

We were supposed to have more time.

I was trying not to freak out at all my unexpected feelings when Hooker began a bouncy waddle dance, raising his crest and singing.

Was he trying to make me laugh?

I kinda thought he was.

The little asshole was being so cute. I patted his chest with my finger, and he danced some more.

It made me smile.

Until my phone rang and the noise sent him off on a swearing tirade. I gave him some more apple and answered the call.

It was Michael.

He didn't know who was getting axed, and I did believe him. He told me he'd have to try and work out transport arrangements. Changing flights, all three of them—including the joy ride in the two-seater Cessna with the crazy pilot—might not be easy. If maybe I could somehow get a lift to Port Hedland . . .

I told him I was happy to stay the full allocated time. Just leave the flights as they are. I didn't even care if I sounded desperate.

He said he'd let me know.

I told him I'd be out of mobile range for the next forty-eight hours. I had a field trip that I couldn't cancel. I didn't tell him it was with Davo to see the stars at midnight . . .

He said he'd have an answer for me when I got back.

I ended the call and Hooker went back to using my laptop as a stage for his silly bird performance. I gave him more scratches. He did more bouncy jumps.

Until I had to call Nisa. As soon as I picked up my phone, Hooker began to screech and swear.

I poured some more seeds out for him as I waited for Nisa to answer my call. She didn't even say hello.

"What did he say?"

"About who's getting fired? Nothing. He doesn't know. I think he's under the impression that he'll be one of them."

Nisa sighed. "No one here knows anything. Everyone's kinda freaked out though. What will we do if it's one of us?"

The fact I hadn't even considered that was a bit of a shock to me. "I, uh, I don't know. God, I haven't even thought about it."

"How can you not?"

I shook my head and shrugged, not that she could see, and let out a huff of air. "I dunno. I guess I was just . . . my first thought was that I didn't want to leave here. Not my job. But here. Michael's trying to get me home earlier, and I didn't consider anything outside of that."

"Fergus," she whispered, stunned. "What the hell? Your job is the reason you're there. Without your job, you wouldn't be there."

Hooker was bored again, so I gave him some more scratches on the head before he could get too rowdy. "I know. And honestly, the fact he wants me to come back looks a lot like my job might be on the line."

"We don't know that yet."

"They'd have a list. Michael might not know who's on it, but the powers that be would."

She was quiet and I could picture her frowning. "I thought you'd be happy about leaving there. Isn't it eleven billion degrees and desolate?"

"No, it's not so bad. I actually like it here."

"You what?"

"I like it here. It's not so bad. I mean, the heat is putrid, but the people are . . ."

"Oh my god."

"Oh my god, what?"

The W word was like a starting gun for Hooker. He waddled in a circle. "What the fuck? What the fuck? What the fuck? What the fuck?"

"You shush with the swearing, mister," I said. Of course, he didn't shut up.

"The people are great. The birds, not so much."

"Fuck, fuck, fuck, fuck, fuck, fuck."

"I'm sorry, Nisa. The psycho chicken's decided not to be quiet."

She laughed. "So is it all the people there that are great, or one person in particular? The reason you were smiling the other day. You *have* met someone there."

"Maybe . . . but it's nothing serious."

"Fergus, you tell me everything."

I laughed. "He's gorgeous. Funny. Sweet. Pretty sure his libido could be measured on the Richter Scale."

She laughed. "You're supposed to be working. Not *working it.*"

"We're just . . . convenient. If you know what I mean."

"So why are you so bummed about coming home?"

Because . . .

Because . . . well, shit.

"Because I don't want to leave him just yet."

"Oh, Fergus."

"I know, I know." I sighed. "He's taking me out to camp overnight at some gorge. Apparently, the stars at midnight are kinda spectacular."

There was a beat of silence. "Well, that doesn't sound convenient. That sounds romantic. Like the most romantic thing I've ever heard, Fergus."

Hooker decided he was bored of everything and that screeching and doing a stompy dance with his wings out was much more entertaining.

"Hooker, please."

"God, he's so loud," Nisa said. "Why is he mad?"

"I'm not paying him any attention. Or the wrong kind of

attention. I don't know. I've tried most of his food already and made him a perch with my broom."

"What does he usually play with?"

"I have no idea. He likes it when I scratch him." I tried to scratch him, but he tried to take off my finger. "Ow. Okay, maybe not. Apparently his old owner, the guy that had him for forty years, said he likes sticks and branches and bark."

Hooker was still doing his angry stomp-dance, squawking, his yellow crest up high. Nisa said something I couldn't hear over the noise.

I stuck my finger in my ear and went into the bathroom. "Sorry, what did you say?"

She laughed. "Does he like bark or Bach? Bark off a tree or Johann Sebastian Bach? I mean, they sound the same."

Hmm. "I don't know. I assumed the tree variety because he said sticks and branches."

"Try music. My dad's birds love music."

Well, it certainly couldn't hurt.

I went to my laptop and ushered cranky-pants Hooker off his dance floor, which he screeched at me for.

"What the fuck? What the fuck? What the fuck?"

"Yeah, I'm sorry."

"You really need to teach him some new words," Nisa said.

"I've tried. He told me to get effed."

Nisa laughed some more.

I hit up YouTube and typed in Bach. Hooker tried to help me type so it took a few goes, but then the music started.

The *Dracula* song. Or Toccata and Fugue in D minor, as it was really called.

And Hooker stopped. He cocked his little head and

watched the laptop screen. Then he extended his wings and began to nod.

Quietly.

"Oh my fucking god, Nisa," I breathed, too scared to make any sudden movements or sounds in case Hooker lost his tiny bird mind again.

She laughed in my ear. "You're welcome."

"You could have told me that before now."

"I rather liked watching him dance on Zoom this morning and how he dropped an array of F-bombs on our boss."

I chuckled. "Well, if Michael wasn't sure who he was going to fire, maybe now he is."

Nisa sighed, all humour gone. "I wish we knew. I don't want to lose anybody. And I don't want to be let go. I love my job and seeing your stupid face."

"Same."

"Well, just enjoy whatever time you have left with Mr Gorgeous."

My heart sank, my belly felt greasy. "Yeah. And on the upside, if I do have to leave early, I get to see your stupid face."

I just hope they can't change my flights.

"I better let you go," I said quietly. "Hooker's enjoying the music, so I'm going to enjoy the first minute of silence I've had."

I could almost feel the smile in her voice. "Talk soon."

I ended the call and sighed.

Why did I feel so bad? Why did the idea of saying goodbye to Davo right now feel so wrong?

Because you like him.

Because you've never met anyone like him.

I stuck out my finger at Hooker's feet and he climbed

on, so I took him and the laptop to the coffee table while I sat on the couch. He danced happily, quietly, and I tried to convince myself that my disappointment was just about the prospect of not finishing this report, of this entire research project not being finished.

Of losing my job, sure.

But the report was important.

The people who the report was about were important.

Davo was important.

I mean, they all were important. I genuinely liked these people.

But Davo . . .

When Orchestral Suite Number 2 came on, Hooker did a twirly waddle dance as he sang a happy tune, making me laugh.

He seemed to like making me laugh. It encouraged him, and he danced more, bounced more, nodded more. I put my feet on the coffee table, and he used my legs as a bridge to jump his way over. He danced up the sofa, back to me, then up onto my belly and my shoulder to the back of the couch and down again.

Gone was the psycho chicken, and in his place was a different cockatoo altogether. Well, he threw out the occasional F-word just to remind me he was still the same bird. But this Hooker was happy and calm. With the simple addition of classical music, the angry and abusive Hooker was gone.

I spent the entire afternoon being entertained by a dancing bird and trying not to think about leaving. That awful, heavy-heart feeling that I had to walk away from someone special.

Later, when there was a knock on the door, I was expecting Truck. But no, it was my someone special. His smile, his bright eyes . . . they took my breath away, and for that one brief second, I forgot all my troubles.

Davo.

How could I be so drawn to him so quickly? How was I ever supposed to walk away from him?

"Hey," he said brightly. "Is it safe to come in?"

CHAPTER ELEVEN

I UNLOCKED MY DOOR AND, trying to act like everything was fine, I refilled Hooker's water. "Sure!"

He stepped into my cabin, looking a bit confused, and of course, Hooker greeted him with a squawk but went back to his music. Davo turned to the sofa where Hooker was now dancing in front of my laptop. Then he turned to me. "What the . . . ?"

I took the water to Hooker and he drank some, then continued to dance and bob his head. "Full choreo and vocals is thirsty work."

Davo, still stunned, laughed. "What? Truck got stuck at work. He'll be here shortly, but he was worried you'd have strangled Hooker by now. He wanted me to come save you."

"Who, from this guy?" I nodded to Hooker. "Nah, he's my little mate now."

Hooker tilted his head to the side and did a circle dance, with his cute little waddle and his mumbling.

Then Truck appeared as if he'd run here, covered in dirt and grease. "Can't hear no one screaming," he said. Then he stopped in his tracks. Both he and Davo just stood there watching as Hooker danced and was, for the most shocking part, quiet.

"What did you do to him?" Truck asked, his eyes wide.

"Nothing. You know how you said his last owner said he liked sticks and branches and bark?"

Truck and Davo nodded.

"Well, it's Bach. Not bark. Johann Sebastian Bach, the composer. Not tree bark." I pointed to my laptop. "It's the fourth time through this playlist. This is Harpsichord Concerto No. 5." I read the name on the YouTube playlist to make sure I got it right. "Look at him dance. He loves it."

"Holy shit," Truck said. "Wally said branches. And sticks. And bark. Like it was all parts of the tree. That's what he told me."

"How did you find this out?" Davo asked. His smile was a little proud, even if I did say so myself.

"Well, after Hooker dropped a cluster of F-bombs on my boss in front of everyone in a Zoom meeting this morning, my friend Nisa asked what he liked. I said bark. She asked if I meant Bach, the composer. So I thought why not try that? I hit Play and he was a different bird." I gestured to the laptop and sighed. "I'm also not allowed to turn it off. And I've done no work today. So there's that. But we had a great day. He's an amazing little guy."

"Do you want to keep—"

"Absolutely not," I replied quickly. I handed Truck the empty lunch box. "Babysitting, yes. Anytime. Periodically, of course."

Davo laughed and clapped Truck's arm. "Nice try."

Truck took a very disgruntled Hooker with him, promising to play more Bach as soon as they got home, and Davo stood in my tiny kitchen, leaning against the counter. He was covered in dust and grease, heat from being outside rolled off him, and his smile made my insides do stupid fluttery things.

"So, you had a good day?" he asked.

"It didn't start out that way. Hooker was in a mood this morning. Enough to send my blood pressure through the roof. I threatened to put him in the fridge."

Davo laughed. "He has that effect on people."

"My boss wasn't impressed."

Davo grimaced, somehow still smiling. "Hooker didn't get you fired, did he?"

Ugh.

About that.

I let out a long breath. "Not Hooker, no."

Davo's smile died. "What?"

"Department budget cuts. My boss isn't sure who's getting let go yet, but he's bringing all field assignments home."

A flurry of expressions crossed his face: confusion, shock, hurt. "What does that mean?"

"He's trying to bring my flights forward."

My heart felt all kinds of heavy.

Davo shook his head. "When?"

I took his hand. I shouldn't feel this way over a guy I'd known for a week. "I don't know. I asked him to leave the flights as they are. It'd save them money. I told him I was happy to stay." I squeezed his hand. "I'm not ready to go yet."

Davo put his head down, his fingers entwining with mine. "I'm not ready yet either."

I cupped his cheek and lifted his face. There was sadness in the blue of his eyes, honesty, and a flicker of fear. I pressed my lips to his. Soft, sweet, a little dusty, sweaty. "I told my boss I'll be out of mobile service for two days, so we should make the most of it."

"You'll *know* if you're leaving in two days? Or you *are* leaving in two days?"

I shrugged. "I'll know. I could be leaving in two days, but we'll know in two days. Hopefully I'm still here for another two weeks."

He frowned but relented a nod. "Two weeks . . ."

He said it like two weeks wasn't long enough either.

I leaned against him, my hips to his, my arms around him, my chin on his shoulder. I wasn't sure what else I could say, so a hug seemed to say all I couldn't.

"You'll get all dirty," he mumbled into my neck. "And I must stink."

"I don't care," I whispered.

We stood there, our arms around each other. This was intimate but not sexual. And it was beautiful.

"Didn't think my work clothes were your thing. Thought you preferred something a little more skirtish."

I chuckled and gave him a squeeze, rubbing his back. "I don't care what you wear. Work pants, shorts, skirt, or nothing at all. Covered in dirt or fresh out of the shower. You're gorgeous in all of the above."

He pulled back, though our hips still pressed together, his hands on my waist. "Is that right?"

I nodded, suddenly nervous. "The most gorgeous man I've ever met."

His rough thumb stroked my jaw. His eyes held me in place, searching. "You don't just like me for the skirts?"

I probably would have made a joke if he hadn't been so guarded, so unsure. He was putting himself out there, braver than me. I shook my head. "No, Davo. I don't care what you wear. As long as you're comfortable and happy, you can wear whatever you want."

He nodded but it was sad, a frown, a furrowed brow. I thought for a second he was going to reply, but with a deep inhale, he shook it off and tried for a smile instead.

"So, we can go camping for two days, huh?"

Our serious conversation was over, for now. I kissed him, soft, lingering. "Better make them good ones."

LATER THAT NIGHT AT DINNER, we'd finished eating and were discussing everything we'd need to pack for our night out camping when the door to the dining hall opened with an abrupt bang.

"Where is he?" a brusque woman's voice yelled.

Oh, dear lord. Someone was in trouble. I didn't dare turn around.

"Where's Fergus?"

I spun in my seat. What the hell?

It was Bronnie. She spotted me and made a beeline toward me, walking much like the front-rower of the union team I made the mistake of sledging once. Believe me, not a mistake I made twice.

The entire dining hall was watching. Even Cookie stuck his head out to stare.

What the hell was I in trouble for? I had no clue. But I tried to stand up. "I can explain," I said, with zero idea of what I was about to explain—it was a life preservation response—when she threw out her arms and picked me up in a crushing bear hug.

"Oh my god," I squeaked.

Everyone was silent, waiting. The only sound in the

huge room was every vertebra in my spine popping like bubble wrap.

She spun me and planted me on my feet, keeping her hands on my shoulders so I didn't fall over. Or collapse.

"Fergus here found the way to shut Hooker up!" she proclaimed. "I've been home for twenty minutes and haven't been sworn at, screeched at, or screamed at." Bronnie turned around to everyone, her hands out like it was the best news she could ever deliver. "Hooker's quiet. In fact, he's singing. And dancing."

Half the hall clapped and cheered. The other half laughed. Davo was on team-laughter. I was so embarrassed I wanted to die.

Bronnie whacked my arm with the back of her hand. "Tell 'em how you did it?"

Everyone waited with bated breath.

"Classical music," Bronnie answered on my behalf, not giving me time to answer at all. "Classical fucking music."

Everyone's eyes went from Bronnie to me. I had to say something. "Er, I found it by accident, really. It was no big deal. But, uh, yeah, he loves it."

"Tell 'em what kind?" Bronnie said. She didn't even give me time to answer that either. "Bach. Not tree bark like we thought Wally meant. But Sebastian Bach. The guy from Skid Row. Didn't even know he did classical."

Oh, good heavens, no. "Well, actually," I began. "It was Johann—"

Bronnie bear-hugged me again until I squeaked. "I could just about kiss you," she said. Then she put me back down and gave Davo an apologetic nod. "But I won't. Sorry."

Davo was too busy laughing to give a shit, apparently.

Bronnie walked out the door with her hands raised, Rocky-style. "No more psycho chicken!"

I sat back down, somewhat violated, more so flustered. "She has great upper body strength. My spine is now pebbles."

Davo was grinning, but at least he wasn't laughing. "I think she's very grateful."

"I got that impression, yeah." I didn't dare look around. "Is everyone still staring?"

Davo glanced behind me and around the hall. "Nope. No one. But come on, let's go."

We got halfway to the door when Creepy stopped us. "Oh, Fergus," he said. "I've been thinking about what you said. You know, about my sculptures and whatnot."

"Oh, yes. Like a website?"

"Well, maybe. Dunno yet. But I'm thinkin' about it."

I couldn't help but smile. "That's good news. I'm happy to help out. Just let me know, okay?"

"Will do. You two have fun out at the gorge."

"We will," Davo replied, and we made it outside before I realised what he'd said.

"Does he know we're going out to the gorge?"

"Pretty sure everyone knows by now," he replied, holding the door to the roadhouse open for me. "Two reasons. First one, well, I was kinda excited and told the fellas at work. Sorry."

I laughed because I certainly wasn't expecting him to say that.

"And two," he held up two fingers. "You gotta tell people when and where you're going out here, and when you'll be back. Especially when you're going off-track."

"Off what?"

"The road."

Oh . . . "Uh, just how much of a track is the road to this place?"

Davo grinned. "Trust me."

"You know, the people who say *trust me* are generally the ones who should not be trusted."

He chuckled and stepped in close, his eyes glinting with humour and daring. "Do you trust me?"

I did. Right or wrong, I trusted him.

"Yes."

"Good. Because where we're going, there isn't really a road. Or a track, for that matter."

"Oh, goodie."

Davo laughed. "Come on, then, let's get what we need. I have stuff I want to do tonight."

"Hi Davo," Junie called out.

"Hey, Junie," he replied.

"Oh, Fergus," she said when she saw me. "Heard you're a bit of a bird whisperer."

Of course she'd heard.

"I didn't do much, actually. And it wasn't my idea. I was on the phone with my friend, and she suggested it. But it worked."

"Well, you're Truck and Bronnie's new favourite person," she said. "Now what can I help you boys with? Need supplies for your trip tomorrow?"

Everyone in town knew, apparently.

"I've lined up some dry ice for the Esky," Davo said. "And we'll be gone for two nights."

Jeesh. Two nights camping off-track in the outback. With like ten of the world's deadliest snakes and no hope of getting to a hospital in time.

"So now would be a really good time to tell you that I've never been camping before in my life, right?" I looked from

Davo to Junie, back to Davo. "That's probably information you should have prior to us going, yeah?"

Davo laughed again. "It's just like staying in your cabin. Except there's no . . . well, there's no cabin. And there's no running water, like from a tap, but there is the gorge. And water. The water's crystal clear."

"It's just like staying in my cabin except there's no cabin? Please tell me we have a tent?"

"How can you see the stars at midnight if you're in a tent?"

Oh dear lord.

"I'd normally just throw in the swag," Davo added. "But if you'd prefer a tent, then we take the tent."

Ugh.

"No, you asked me to trust you, so I will. We do it your way. Just out of interest, how big is the swag?"

Davo's gaze darted to Junie, then to me. "Well, it's a single."

I stared at him and ignored Junie's laugh as she walked off down the back of the store. "Jeez, Davo. Not sure Junie needed to know that."

He shrugged, unbothered. "Pretty sure she already knew."

Junie came back and handed over an empty chip box to Davo. "Here ya go."

He looked inside and laughed, then handed the box to me. In the bottom of the box was another pack of condoms.

Oh dear god.

I sighed, defeated. "Is nothing private here?"

Davo gave me an apologetic shrug, but his smile told me he was far from sorry.

Then, just when I thought it couldn't get any more

embarrassing, Junie added, "Don't have any of that lube though."

I almost died. "Oh my god."

"Got some Mobil engine lubrication in the workshop if you need it," Bill joked as he walked out from the back. He'd clearly heard the whole conversation.

Sweet mother of god.

"Don't be silly," Junie said, shaking her head.

Davo snorted. "We're not Transformers, Bill."

How was this even real?

I put my hand up. "I'd just like to quote Hooker when I say, 'what the fuck, what the fuck, what the fuck?'"

Davo burst out laughing and took my arm. "This way."

We bought some bacon and eggs, juice, bread, sausages, some fruit, and at my insistence, a packet of red frogs. Junie took pity on me as she processed the sale and refrained from any more talk about sex and opted only for a cheery wave as we left.

"Well, that whole transaction was horrifying," I mumbled as we walked down to his cabin.

He just smiled. "There are very few secrets here. And Junie and Bill are cool with just about everything. They're kinda like the cool aunt and uncle who were absolutely stoners in the 70s."

"I guess."

"If it really bothers you, I can ask them to cool it."

I sighed. "Nah. It's fine. I'm just not used to it." And in all honesty, it wasn't something I'd have to get used to.

I had to wonder if that's where Davo's mind went too because he was quiet until we reached his cabin. He handed the box over to me, took out his keys.

I stood on his little porch, the rainbow spinner still in the breezeless evening. The sunset was being a bit of a show-off: pinks, oranges, and deep purples. "It's so pretty here," I mused. "Never thought I'd ever think the desert could be pretty."

Davo slid open the door but turned to me. "You might wanna watch yourself. First, helping with Hooker, and then offering to help Creepy. Might make yourself a local. You should be careful. This place has a way of collecting people."

I wish . . .

And just like that, the realisation that my days here were numbered was back at the front of my mind.

I knew he thought the same because he frowned as he took the box. "Don't think about it," he whispered. "Instead, think about what you're going to do to me all night. I don't have to be up too early in the morning, so you can stay."

I sighed and followed him inside, and as soon as he put the box down, I cupped his face and kissed him before I pulled him in for a hug. He slid his arms around me and hugged me just as tight. And after a long moment, he sighed and pulled back, keeping his hands at my waist. "I was going to sew up that skirt tonight, but honestly, I think I'd rather stay right here."

I chuckled and kissed him. "You do your skirt. I'll go get my laptop and do the work I didn't get done today because of a tantrum-throwing bird-toddler."

He studied my eyes. "Are you sure?"

I gave a nod and another kiss. "And I'll pack a bag so I can stay all night, and we can leave in the morning whenever we get out of bed."

He smirked. "I think we're going to need to be more specific with a time."

I chuckled. "Or we'd never leave?"

"Exactly."

"Well, I wouldn't mind."

"Me either. But I really want you to see the gorge, the stars. And I'd be lying if I said having you to myself for two days isn't the main reason."

Smiling, I put my forehead to his. My heart was pushing me to say things my brain wasn't ready for. "I'll go get my laptop. Then I'm all yours for two days."

So that's what we did.

Davo sat at his sewing machine, the hum of it and how he mumbled to himself as he sewed a great distraction, but I did manage to get some work done.

It had been an eventful day, and I was tired. But most of all, sitting in Davo's cabin with him, while he did his thing and I did mine, was a real peaceful, easy feeling.

It was so easy.

The TV was on, but it was only quiet background noise. He'd been drowning in metres of pink tulle but had somehow managed to tame it. "I'm almost done," he said. I still had my laptop open but hadn't written anything in a while. He must have noticed.

"Do I get to see the finished product?" I asked.

"Not until tomorrow."

"Ooh, the grand reveal!"

He made an unsure face. "I hope you like it."

"I'm sure I will. But Davo, it's something *you've* always wanted. So as long as you like it, that's all that matters."

His whole face softened. "Just remember that this is my first attempt and it's more of a prototype."

"Like a first draft," I said, gesturing to my laptop.

"Exactly." He folded some leftover tulle. "It's a different type of fabric than I'm used to. The stretch and pull are different."

"Hmm, stretch and pull. Two of my favourite things."

He chuckled, then nodded to my work. "How'd you go?"

"Yeah, pretty good. If I do have to leave in a few days, I have enough information so I can patch something together." I closed my laptop and slid it onto the coffee table. "I have the whole next shift of fly in, fly outers that are coming this week that I won't get to interview now. And I wanted to speak to someone about maybe getting a look at the mine. The actual worksite. Just so I can appreciate what it is you guys do." I looked at him and shrugged. "I don't know what will happen to this report now anyway. Or my job." I sighed. "Sorry. I didn't mean to be a downer."

"It's okay," he said, leaving the sewing machine and coming over to sit beside me. He took my hand in his. "What will you do if you're one of the ones let go?"

"Dunno. There're a lot of research agencies, but not many that apply to my background. Certainly wouldn't move to Canberra to fulfil the politicians' 'research data,' that's for damn sure."

Davo laughed.

"I used to do copy-editing in college," I said. "Mostly for websites and stuff. I could do it at night and it paid okay. Well, it paid for rice and beer, which was basically my staple university diet."

He chuckled. "Sounds familiar."

"God, what will I do if I'm fired?" There I was still more concerned with having to leave Davo than thinking about employment contingency plans. I hadn't really thought about it since Nisa mentioned it earlier. I sighed. "I would miss Nisa. She's my work-wife."

He blinked and stared. "Your what?"

I snorted. "My work-wife. My bestie at work. We gossip

and bitch about everyone. Don't you have someone at work you just click with better than the others?"

"Well, yeah. Probably Truck and Gibbo. A good mate of mine left a few years ago. He did his time at the mine, made his money, and got out. Most of 'em do. He moved up to Darwin. He still calls every so often."

"Were you two more than just mates?"

Davo laughed. "Nah. Nothing like that."

"What was his name?"

"Gary. But his nickname was Sensor Light."

"Why?"

"Because he only ever worked when someone walked past."

I burst out laughing. "Oh my god. The nicknames. How come you don't have one?"

He shrugged. "I'm just Davo."

"Anyone ever call you David?"

He shook his head. "Only my mother."

"Do your parents still live in Perth?" He'd said he'd grown up there . . .

He nodded. "I don't see them too often. Usually around Christmas. They don't exactly like me being gay. And they certainly don't like the skirts."

I frowned. "I'm sorry."

He gave me a sad smile. "Me too. I found my family here though."

I cupped his cheek and kissed him, soft and sweet. "I'm glad."

"Me too." He held my gaze for a long moment. "I'm sorry you've got work troubles, and I'm really bummed that your stay here might be cut short."

"Same." I let my head fall back and I stared at this gorgeous, rugged man in his pretty skirt. "I don't want to think about work, or the fact I might lose my job, or the fact I could be leaving in a few days. I just . . . I just don't want to think about any of it."

Especially the leaving part.

"Then let's not think about it. We've got two days of camping away. Let's just enjoy them." He stood up in front of me and he slowly hitched his skirt up his thigh. "I've got something that'll take your mind off your worries. If you suck it properly, that is."

I burst out laughing. But oh boy, was he ever right.

Chapter Twelve

I doubted Davo had ever slept in past 5:30am. But the upside of this was that his ute was packed and ready to go by the time I dragged myself out of bed at 6:30am.

"Hey, sleeping beauty," he said, grinning at me from the back of his ute where it was parked out the front of his cabin. He was wearing shorts and an old T-shirt, plus his work boots and a cap.

I'd never seen him wear a cap before. He looked very blokey, very gorgeous.

"Hey, handsome," I said.

"Morning," someone replied, a hand popping up from behind the ute.

Davo laughed and shoved that poor someone. "Think he was talking to me."

Gibbo's smiling face appeared. "Mornin', Fergus. Hate to rush ya and all, but someone here's a bit excited to get going."

I snorted. "Yeah, okay. Message received and understood."

"We'll grab brekkie on the way out," Davo said as I went inside.

God, he was keen to leave.

I had the quickest shower of my life, forwent a shave, grabbed my bag, and threw it to Davo. He appeared to have some kind of intricate packing thing going on that I wasn't going to infringe upon. His work ute had massive white toolboxes that lined both sides of the tray back. The sides were up, and I could see canisters of water, a jerrycan of fuel, a huge first aid kit, and a gas cylinder. Not to mention the fire extinguisher and two spare tyres fitted to the under-carriage.

"Just so you know, if there's a zombie apocalypse, I'm on your team."

Davo grinned. "Gotta be prepared."

"For the *Hunger Games*?"

He laughed. "Out here, it'd be more like *Mad Max*."

"I'm not comforted by that."

Gibbo laughed. "You two have fun."

Davo closed the sides of his ute and locked up his house. "Not taking your laptop?"

"Nope. I am absolutely not contactable for two days."

"I do have a satellite phone."

"My boss doesn't need to know that."

He grinned. "You ready?"

"Not at all, but excited to do it anyway."

We drove the ute up to the hall and had a quick bite for breakfast, and Davo grabbed a few of the sandwiches and some fruit the kitchen put out for anyone to take, should they need to hit the road early or got in late.

"Should we be taking those?" I asked.

"Sure. I asked Cookie to make a few extra. And what

doesn't get eaten during the day gets toasted for the night shift. Not much goes to waste here."

"Oh, that's good."

Davo handed me the sandwiches to hold as we walked out. "You're always worried about the workers," he said. "I like that." When we got to the ute, he nodded to the road-house. "Last call for Sprite or gum."

"Or engine oil for lube."

Davo laughed and got in behind the steering wheel. "Packed my own, thanks."

As we drove out, I couldn't help but notice how excited Davo was. "You're really looking forward to this, aren't you?"

"Yes," he said, shifting in his seat a little as if he was nervous. But his smile was something else. "I am. I love going out to this spot, and I never dreamed that I'd ever get to take anyone . . . you know, like a date type of thing." He shrugged. "It's exciting for me and kind of a big deal. Sorry if I rushed you a bit this morning."

I held my hand out over the centre console, palm up, and waited for him to slip his hand into mine. I threaded our fingers. "It's kind of a big deal for me too."

We drove past the turn-off to the landing strip on the left—well, I think that was it—and we drove for about another kilometre when Davo began to slow down. He put his blinker on to turn right, and then I noticed streetlights up ahead. Out here, in the middle of nowhere.

"Why the lights?" But then a sign came into view. "Ah."

Pannalego Mine.

But he was slowing down? "Oh my god, are we going there?"

Davo laughed. "You said you wanted to see it. We won't stop or get out. But I'll show you where I work."

He took his hand back so he could change gears, and it was ridiculous how excited I was to see a whopping hole in the ground.

One thing about the mining industry was that they spent money. The road was only dirt, but it was wide, very smooth, very well maintained. I'd driven on billion-dollar freeways that weren't that good.

So maybe it wasn't money. Maybe it was because every single employee was an engineer of some kind, and they had all the equipment at their disposal to make it perfect.

We passed a gate where Davo flashed his card. The guy waved . . . no, it wasn't just a guy. It was Gus, one of the fly-in, fly-out guys I'd spoken to a few days ago.

And about a hundred metres later, there were parking bays and buildings and huge sheds. It was like another entire town. "These are the admin blocks, training centre, the tyre bay, workshop, fuel depot up the back."

We kept on driving.

"Up over there is processing and loading . . ." He continued to give me a guided tour as we drove, but then we turned at some markers on the road, and after a few hundred metres, the whole landscape changed.

The wide roads were busy. Utes, trucks, and not just normal ones but the biggest trucks I'd ever seen. They looked like giant Tonka trucks. Sure, I'd seen them on TV and in pictures before, but never up close.

"Holy shit."

Davo laughed, and I didn't care that I felt like a kid on a school excursion. He drove down and around the huge winding road and pulled off to another cluster of buildings where utes and trucks were parked. "This is where I work," he said. "Well, mostly. Sometimes I'm up in the main buildings. Sometimes I'm down in the hole."

"The hole?"

Smiling, he drove out past the buildings along a much thinner road to what appeared to be a viewing bay. A lookout above what was a huge freaking hole in the ground. Those huge-ass Tonka trucks drove along the edges like ants in those ant farms I had as a kid.

It was mindboggling. The scale of it had to be seen to be believed. And there was so, so much red dirt.

"It looks like we're on Mars," I said.

Davo chuckled. "Seen enough?"

I nodded. "Thank you for bringing me here."

"You're welcome."

We drove back out, soon on the main road once again. The landscape for hundreds of miles was flat and red, speckled with green shrubs and trees that clearly didn't need much water to survive.

"Whatcha thinking?"

I must have been too quiet for too long. "Oh, sorry. I was just thinking how it's all so . . ." I gestured to the vast openness out my window and the windscreen.

"Flat? Boring?"

"No. It's beautiful. It's crazy to me. If someone had asked me a month ago what was the most beautiful part of Australia, I'd probably point them in the direction of the beaches or the rainforests. Never would have even considered this." He was smiling at me, and I ignored how it made my heart swell. "The early morning sun makes it all look so soft, almost pastel in colour."

This time Davo held his hand out and I took it, relishing in the warmth and the strength of his grip. Savouring the butterflies and thrill it gave me.

About half an hour later we passed a sign that said Yillinali, the closest town, was another fifty-five kilometres away, but then Davo began to slow down and he turned left off the main road.

"You weren't kidding when you said it was a track."

He grinned. "This is good. Gonna get a bit bumpier yet."

"Awesome."

It did get bumpier, but it also got greener.

"The trees are different. They're taller," I noted. "So I'm guessing there's groundwater along here."

Davo seemed pleased by this. "Very observant." He pointed out his driver's window. "There's a creek along there. Natural springs. You'll see. Not far now."

About thirty minutes later, there was a bit of a flattened area, like a parking bay, and Davo pulled up to a stop. "Come take a squiz at this."

I stepped out of the air-conditioned ute and into the heat but followed him down a rough path to what I could now see was a ledge. Below us was a deep gorge, a canyon, with sheer orange-red walls on the sides and a blue-green river at the bottom. Trees and ferns sprung from crevices, bright green against the red.

"Oh my god," I breathed.

"Spectacular, huh?"

I nodded. "Davo, it's breathtaking."

"It's got decent water in it from the rains."

I looked around. "Is this where we're stopping?"

He grinned. "Nope. We got a ways to go yet."

I was even more excited now. I took a bunch of photos on my phone, and we were soon back in the welcome air conditioning, driving further down the track.

After a bit, the track seemed to come to a natural end—a well-used parking area—and I thought we'd be stopping, but nope. "That's where the tourists come to," he said as he took us along what was not really a track at all. Maybe a fire trail that was used once a year? "We'll go somewhere more private."

It was bumpy, but Davo took it slow, and he was a very capable driver. And it was a good thirty minutes later when he rounded a cluster of gum trees and pulled up in the shade.

In front of us was a watering hole, fenced on one side by a jagged red wall of rock. Red rock and red sand led down to the water. Ferns, reeds, trees, and grasses decorated the whole area.

"Davo, what is this place?" I whispered.

I feared if I spoke too loudly or if I blinked, it would disappear like a mirage.

"It's a billabong. It pockets off the gorge."

"It's . . ." I let out an amazed sigh. "It's gorgeous."

His grin almost paled in comparison.

Almost.

"Come on, let's get our camp set up and we can take a swim."

Camp, as it turned out, was two camping chairs, a small gas BBQ, and a swag, which he put up on top of the cage rack on the roof of his ute.

"What if I roll off?" I asked. "Or forget where I am and get up to take a leak and take a two-metre step to the ground."

"Well," he replied. "We can keep it on the ground, but I thought maybe to avoid any snakes or lizards—"

I stared at him, waiting for him to tell me he was joking.

He didn't.

"The two-metre fall in the middle of the night is fine."

Davo laughed and reassured me with his hand on my arm. "You'll be fine. I'll keep hold of you all night."

I pulled him in for a quick, hard kiss. "You better."

"Wanna go for a swim?"

"Hell yes. I'll need you to sunscreen me up first though, please."

Davo pulled off his shirt and tossed his cap into the back of the ute, then unlaced his boots. The shorts he was wearing were the nylon football kind, good for swimming, easy to dry.

I had to change into my gym shorts. The very short, tight gym shorts.

Davo took one look at me, the sunscreen tube in his hand forgotten. "Are those the . . . the gym shorts you talked about?"

I turned, showed off my arse, and did a bit of a squat. "Yep. Great stretch, great fit. Don't you think?"

He was dazed. "I, um . . . uh . . . holy hell."

"You okay?"

"No, they're obscene. And fucking hot. You really wore those to the gym? Like out in public?"

"Yep."

"Just how much shower-room sex at the gym did you have?"

I laughed. "Jealous?"

"Hell yes. I want to see you get all sweaty, doing squats and lifts."

I gave him my back so he could apply some sunscreen. "Oh, you want a private viewing?"

He massaged the sunscreen on my skin, stepping in close. "I want more than that."

Hmm. I leaned back into his touch. "Keep going like that and we'll see how much stretch these shorts have."

He finished sunscreening me, then slapped my arse. Hard. "Don't tease me." He lathered some sunscreen on his shoulders and on his face, grinned at me like a doofus, and walked out into the water.

I applied my sunscreen with a little more finesse.

He was waist-deep already. "Hurry up."

"See this white skin? See how pasty it is? I will fry."

Grinning, he sank under the surface, coming up and raking his hair back, looking sexy as hell.

When I was sure I'd adequately sunscreened myself, I walked into the water.

"Don't splash too much," Davo said. "Attracts the crocodiles." I shrieked, and he cracked up laughing. "I'm kidding! There are no crocs here."

"Davo!" I grabbed my dick. "I peed a little!"

He laughed so hard I thought he might burst something.

I trudged forward, splashing him and throwing my arms around his neck and kissing him. He wrapped me up and took me under. The water was cool, his mouth was hot, his hold was tight, and we floated.

It was magic.

WE ATE our sandwiches at lunch, sitting in the camping chairs under the tree. It must have been ten degrees cooler where we were. The sounds of birds and crickets and frogs was a symphony.

"This is amazing," I said. "I cannot believe this place even exists."

"There's quite a few gorges like this all over the Pilbara region."

I sighed. "It's so . . . peaceful. I don't even know if that's the right word. It's more than peaceful." I shook my head, not really making much sense. "It feels old and wise, spiritual. I dunno. That probably sounds crazy."

Davo stared at me, a serene look on his face. "Makes perfect sense. This place *is* old. Millions of years. We are but a speck of dust in the time of this place."

I sighed and looked back out over the billabong.

We are but a speck of dust in the time of this place.

"It's hard to get your head around, isn't it?" he added. "Geologists have dated the zircon found in this part of Australia back three billion years. Three billion. I can't even fathom that length of time or imagine what the earth looked like."

Three billion years? "Way too early for dinosaurs."

"Earth would have been nothing but a fiery, volcanic planet, rivers of lava, that kind of thing." He sighed. "And now here we are, three billion years later, and I'm lucky enough to exist at the same time as you."

I didn't know what to say.

I could barely speak.

My eyes and the back of my nose burned, but I didn't want to cry. "I reckon I'm pretty lucky to exist at the same time as you too."

Davo's smile disappeared into a frown. "Did I upset you just now?"

I shook my head and laughed at myself. "Only because it was the most beautiful thing anyone has ever said to me."

He leaned over and beckoned me to meet him halfway for a kiss. "Any guy who hasn't said sappy, beautiful shit to you was a fool."

His eyes told me he wanted to say more, but he chewed his bottom lip instead. He leaned back in his chair, stretched his legs out, pulled his cap down a bit, and closed his eyes.

His muscular chest, his broad shoulders, the line of his neck. His jaw, his stubble, his pink lips, the way his cap cast a shadow across his cheekbones.

"You're really very gorgeous, you know that?"

A smile formed on his lips, but he never pulled his cap up.

"You can be manly as hell. Like right now, all masculine, no shirt, footy shorts, unshaven. Then you can wear a skirt with such confidence, it leaves me speechless."

His smile pulled up on one side and he moved his cap back so he could see me. "Which do you prefer?"

"Both. Equally. I've told you before. I find both equally attractive. Both turn me on. But you carry yourself a little different when you wear a skirt. Not out in public but at home. You sway a little like you feel sexy, and that, you feeling good about yourself, is the sexiest thing."

His eyes met mine and he stared before he sucked his bottom lip in between his teeth, again, like he wanted to say something but wouldn't.

Instead, he said, "Did you want to see my new skirt? The pink tulle one?"

"Hell yes, I do."

He grinned, nervous and excited. "Okay." He shot up out of his chair and went to the ute. I didn't turn around because I wanted the surprise and to make this a big deal for him.

He'd always wanted to make this skirt.

It was special to him, so I had to keep that in mind.

I heard the rustle of fabric and he swore a few times, but after a beat of silence, he said, "Okay, close your eyes."

I covered my eyes with my hands and waited . . . and waited.

"You can look now."

Davo stood a few metres in front of me, nervous but brave. The skirt wasn't a tutu, exactly. Same fabric as one and many layers, but a bit longer. It didn't stick straight out like a tutu, but it sat neatly out from his thighs, a thick pink ribbon tied around his waist.

I didn't know what to expect, really. But I didn't expect that.

"Holy shit," I whispered, getting to my feet. "Davo."

"You like it?"

I shook my head. "Love it. It's beautiful. You're beautiful."

He ducked his head and smiled, his hand flattening down the fabric on his thigh.

I lifted his hand to my lips and kissed his knuckles.

He ducked his head again, his smile shy. He'd almost curtsied.

Wow, what a reaction.

So I stood tall, my other hand behind my back, and lifted his hand above our heads, leading him into a pirouette. He laughed as he turned, and when he faced me again, he was grinning, his cheeks pink with blush.

I pulled him against me. "Beautiful."

He might not have been able to say the words on the tip of his tongue earlier, but my god, when he kissed me, I sure could taste them.

CHAPTER THIRTEEN

WE SPENT the afternoon swimming and making out, talking and laughing. As the sun got lower, Davo wanted me to see the sunset from the top of the rock formation at the side of the billabong. It wasn't exactly far, and it wasn't a difficult climb, though I was very aware of how far we were from medical help should one of us fall.

"Are you looking up my skirt?"

I laughed. "No. I'm too busy trying not to die. I hope you know that if you fall and get hurt, I won't be able to get us out of here," I said as we climbed.

He laughed as he reached the top, then turned to help pull me up. "You'd do just fine. And anyway, I wouldn't do anything to put us at risk."

It really wasn't that high up, and getting down would be easy. "Yeah, I know. I'm just a city boy prone to exaggeration and pessimism."

He put the bag he was carrying on the ground and pulled out a blanket, propping up two cans of Diet Coke. "It was all I had in the Esky."

I kissed his cheek. "It's perfect. You really thought of everything."

This platform gave us a perfect view of the sunset, apparently. Above the trees and rocks, but also a perfect view of the billabong and further up into the gorge.

I took more photos, knowing damn well they didn't do any of it justice. And I took more photos of Davo in his pink tulle skirt as he stood with the incredible view behind him, but also when I sat on the blanket and captured him against the sky. He had his arms out, the ribbon on his skirt tousled in the breeze, and so god help me, it was the most beautiful thing I'd ever seen. It was a little overcast, but the sunset just added matching hues of pink to the clouds behind him as well.

"Hey, handsome," I said. "Turn around for me."

He did, and I clicked a few more photos, wanting every memory of him I could capture before I had to leave.

He fell into his spot beside me and clinked his can of Diet Coke to mine. "Cheers."

"Cheers. And thank you for bringing me here."

"And you haven't even seen the stars at midnight yet."

I'd almost forgotten about the reason for us coming out here. "Not sure I'll be able to stay awake," I said.

"I'll keep you awake." He nudged me with his shoulder. "Now, shh. The show's about to start."

The show he was referring to was the sun meeting the horizon, and it was spectacular.

Pinks, oranges, yellows filled the sky but also spilled across the red earth, splashing colour on every surface. We sat, shoulders touching, taking in every change of colour as the sun got lower and lower.

I couldn't believe I'd have missed all this if it weren't for Davo. I'd have never sat in the middle of the desert near a hidden oasis watching a sunset hit almost every colour on the spectrum.

"Thank you," I murmured. "For sharing this with me." This is the second sunset he'd shown me. I needed the reminder to stop for a second and appreciate the things we so easily overlooked.

"You're very welcome." He planted a soft, wet kiss on my lips. "But we should get back to camp before it gets too dark. You hungry?"

"I am a bit, yeah."

The sky was now purples and dark blues. We had heaps of time to climb back down, and Davo hooked up the gas BBQ plate. In just a few seconds, he had sausages cooking. The smell made me realise just how hungry I was.

After dinner, Davo moved the ute out from under the trees and he made sure the swag was all set up. His grinning face appeared at the top. "You ready to climb up?"

"Need me to bring anything else up?"

"Nah. I have condoms, lube, and a towel. Oh, throw me up a bottle of water out of the Esky."

I did that and followed him up, climbing into the tray back of the ute first, then onto the cage rack. It was a bit of a tight fit, but I managed to squeeze myself up.

"Those shorts are my new favourite thing," he said. "You know I could probably sew you some more. A fraction tighter though."

I chuckled and lay down next to him. He was still wearing his new skirt. "These shorts are tight enough."

He went straight for the kill—cupped my balls and gave me a long, slow pull. "I've seen the outline of this all day," he murmured. "Surprised we made it to nightfall."

I pushed him onto his back and knelt over him, my hands beside his head, one leg between his thighs. I wanted something different with him tonight. My heart needed something more.

No pummelling him into the mattress, no desperate, hard fucking. "I'm going to take my time with you tonight," I murmured before kissing him, teasing him with my tongue. "Slow, deep. And your skirt stays on."

He groaned. "Are you gonna make me beg?"

I wedged my other leg between his and pushed his thighs apart. "You'll do more than beg."

By the time I had him ready for me, he was writhing with want. The tulle was pushed up against his belly, his hands lost in the fabric. I pushed his knees up, slid my sheathed cock across his hole, and slowly pressed in.

I lay over him, my eyes lost in his, watching every flicker of emotion as I entered him. His mouth fell open, his eyes rolled back, and he gasped and whined.

I kissed him, not stopping until I was fully seated inside him, only to pull back a little and slide back in.

Davo's fingers clawed at my back, my arse, grabbing onto me desperately. But I kept the same slow pace, savouring every sound he made.

I kissed him, plunging my tongue into his mouth, in complete control of his body.

This wasn't fucking. This wasn't a frantic romp, chasing orgasms and nothing else. This was making love.

Because you love him.

You're in love with him.

This perfect man.

"God, Davo," I whispered.

He raised his hips more, his legs relaxed, and I pushed in deeper, longer. He let his arms fall from around me, fully surrendering his body to me, letting me have him how I wanted him.

I slid my arms under his shoulders, holding him to me as I sank to my balls, over and over. He'd smeared precome between us, his cock rock-hard, his body pliable, and I was so far inside him.

"Fergus," he groaned. "Oh, Fergus. So good. Just like that. Fuck yes."

So I thrust a little harder, again and again, until his fists gripped the cage above his head, his body strung tight. And he came, shooting streams of come onto his skirt, chest, and belly.

I thrust harder, prolonging his orgasm and finding my own. Pleasure exploded from my bones, ripping through me like a bomb. I bucked into him one last time, roaring with ecstasy, and I filled the condom deep inside him.

He draped his arms around me, pulling me close and kissing me. Deep and gentle until my senses returned. Then I buried my face in his neck while he drew circles on my back, peppering kisses on all the skin he could reach.

"You okay?" he asked eventually.

"Hm. You?"

He chuckled, his body vibrating underneath me. "I don't think I've ever been this okay."

Reluctantly, I pulled out and wrapped my arms around him. I nuzzled into his neck, sleepy and sated.

Utterly boneless.

And very much in love.

"Hey," he whispered. "Don't fall asleep."

I tried to keep my eyes open. "Wassup? You okay? Need anything?"

He smiled, sliding his palm to my cheek. "Look up."

I turned my head and had to blink away my tiredness. The entire sky was alight with millions of stars. The Milky

Way looked like it had ripped the sky open, letting in shades of purple and blue and orange.

"Holy shit."

Davo laughed. "Isn't it something else?"

I'd never seen anything like it. No picture had ever done it justice. It honestly didn't seem real. I reached for his hand and squeezed. "Oh my god," I breathed.

"Crazy to think all those stars are up there, light-years away," he mused. "And here we are, looking back at them."

"You know, I might have said you were the most beautiful thing I'd ever seen, but that?" I gestured to the sky. "I think this might be better. Sorry."

He laughed. "Have you ever told me I was the most beautiful thing you'd ever seen?"

"Pretty sure I have. I mean, I've thought it a lot."

He laughed again, bringing our joined hands to his lips for a kiss.

And we laid there, not speaking, just holding hands, trying to count the stars.

THE NEXT MORNING something was different in me.

I was different.

Something had shifted inside me. The way I saw the world, the way I saw Davo, the way I felt.

I was in love with him, and as we spent most of the day swimming, eating, lazing in the shade, making out, doing a bit of hiking and laughing, I had to wonder if I should tell him.

Considering I was leaving any day, would it be better if he knew? Or would it only serve to hurt him more when I left?

I didn't know.

What would I prefer? To never know, or to know and have to leave anyway?

As the day became night, I was only more confused.

We didn't make love this time, instead simply content to lie in each other's arms and stare at the magnificent night sky.

The feeling of insignificance, of being a mere speck of dust in the universe, weighed on my mind. Maybe Davo was fighting the same internal war. The way he clung to me, held me, and needed to be held kinda told me he was.

The next morning at breakfast and as we packed up, we were both kinda quiet. The weight of leaving was heavy. The weight of leaving Davo for good was almost unbearable.

"You ready to go back?" he asked.

I shook my head. "No."

He nodded. "Same." He held out his hand, which I took, and he pulled me against him and we stood there, holding each other until we couldn't put it off any longer.

The drive back to town started out quiet too, though we held hands over the centre console. But then Davo turned the radio on and we sang '80s songs really loudly and terribly all the way home.

We were smiling as we drove past the roadhouse, and Davo dropped me off at my cabin. I leaned over and kissed him. "See ya at lunch."

The promise of a shower lured me inside. I didn't check my phone or laptop, opting for the use of a proper bathroom instead, wanting to put off the inevitable for as long as possible. I took my time, scrubbing two days of dirt and billabong water off me, shaved and brushed my teeth properly, and felt like a new human.

There was a knock on my door. It was Davo. "Hey, you're early," I said, then I realised he wasn't smiling, and he was wearing shorts and his work boots. "What's wrong?"

"Come on. There's a town meeting in the hall."

A town meeting?

"What's wrong?"

"There's talk of shutting down the mine."

CHAPTER FOURTEEN

THERE WERE MORE people in the hall than I'd ever seen there. Including two men in expensive suits who stood in the corner by the stage.

Davo and I came in just as everyone was getting settled. He went to the front of the hall, while I stood by the wall at the side. Davo spoke with Gibbo, Truck and Bronnie, JC and Chappy. The permanent residents. It looked serious. I saw him glance at the two suits every so often.

My stomach was somewhere near my feet.

Junie snuck in and came by to stand next to me. "What's going on?" I asked.

"The powers that be reckon Pannalego's losing feasibility," she murmured.

"What does that mean?" I asked.

"Profitability isn't where it once was or where they want it."

Fucking hell.

"What does that mean? For the town?"

She shrugged. "Mines close. It happens."

Yeah, I understood that nothing lasted forever. "But what about you guys?"

She gave me a grim smile.

My stomach knotted, greasy and slick.

The two men took to the stage and called for everyone's attention. They spoke of the latest feasibility study, life-cycle assessments, resources, commodity supercycles, extraction viability, economic markets, export costs, metric tonnage, blah, blah, blah.

Everyone listened. Davo seemed to understand, but it was all financial keywords to me.

"Pannalego has been in operation for ten years," they said. "They'd hoped for longer, but it's been a good run."

Now *that* I understood.

They were going to close it down.

The owners of Pannalego had applied for a new licence, a new site, eighty kilometres southwest of our current location. Drill tests were positive, and prospects were looking extremely good. It was going to be a big site, with plans for double what they were running now.

They were happy to extend employment for all currently contracted staff. New contracts, of course. With one major change to the current arrangement.

"We will not be looking at maintaining permanent residents," they said. "All positions will be fly in, fly out."

There was absolute silence in the room. Davo's face . . . I'd never forget it.

"After extensive studies into the well-being and living options for people in the mining sector, the latest reports have shown that fly in, fly out is the most sustainable employment choice and therefore . . ."

Almost every head in that hall turned to me, Davo included. Junie, Truck, Gibbo.

The look on Davo's face.

Oh my god.

They thought my report had something to do with this? Davo thought I had a hand in this?

I put my hand to my heart. "Me? I haven't even finished my report, let alone submitted it." I shook my head.

The suit who'd done the most talking looked me up and down. "Ah, you're the academic who was granted research permission."

"Fergus Galloway," I replied. "No report has been submitted—"

"I'm sure we can discuss this afterwards," he said brusquely. He turned back to the crowd. "Pannalego Mine has been given two years to wrap up. All contracts will be honoured and seen . . ."

Blah, blah, fucking blah.

They believed the length of notice and full disclosure and not a memo with a month's notice was worthy of merit.

Maybe it was.

But I was too busy trying to regulate my breathing. That nausea was swiftly moving into anger.

When the meeting was done, almost all of the fly-in, fly-out staff left. It was still too early for lunch, and given Cookie was sitting with the other permanents, I wasn't sure if there'd even be a lunch service today.

I went straight to suit one and suit two. "I absolutely did not submit any report," I said, interrupting them. I was past caring. I also didn't care who heard me. In fact, I hoped everyone heard.

"We never said it was your report," Suit One said.

"Can I ask to see the report to which you're referring? Because those findings are either outdated, incomplete, or biased. I'm sure it's properly cited, right?"

Suit Two gave me a polite-yet-hostile smile. "Not that we have to disclose any information to you, but I can assure you the report was legitimate."

"I've been here for less than two weeks, and I can tell you the permanent residents of this town are the backbone of what makes it work. They are a constant in a revolving door of staff, and when I first got here, I thought originally that it was Cookie, Junie, and Bill who kept this place running. And they do, but it's not that simple. This *machine* has many moving parts. Like all operations, some cogs are a little bigger than others, but it takes all the cogs to make it work. Every single person here is a part of that machine, but none are more so important than the permanents. They are the stabilisers of the machine that makes you money."

The two suits looked at me and I realised then they didn't even know who Cookie, Junie, or Bill were.

I shook my head. "You don't even care. These people right here are some of the best people. Good, salt-of-the-earth people who have kept your business running for a decade, and you don't even know their fucking names."

Davo was behind me then, his hand on my lower back. "Hey."

I turned to him. "Why aren't you pissed off? They're taking away your home." I pointed to the ground. "This is your home. Fight for it!"

Davo gave the slightest shake of his head.

No.

Just like that. No.

I looked at Gibbo, at Truck and Bronnie. At Cookie and JC.

There was no fight in any of them.

I met Davo's eyes. "So that's it? It's over?"

"Fergus," he said gently. "The decision's made. Mines close all the time. The mining camps close with them."

"So what am I even doing here? What difference can I make when they don't even care? Their reports would've been done by someone paid by the mining corporation to give them the answer they want, to justify decisions already made." I was so mad, I could have spit. "It's bullshit and you know it!"

Then one of those fucking suits mumbled something and the other one smiled.

I spun on my heel, fists closed and jaw clenched. I made one step in their direction and Davo stepped in and wrapped his arms around me and carried me outside.

He only put me down when he'd reached the end of the ramp, and as soon as my feet were on the ground, he took my arm and led me toward the shade of the undercover bay at the roadhouse.

His grip on me loosened, but he never let go. "You okay now?"

I was still so mad. "How can you not care?"

"Of course I care. We all do. This is our home. But it's not as black and white as you think."

"Then explain it to me. Because you said you'd never do the fly-in, fly-out thing, so *explain* it to me."

He sighed. "We're employees here. That's all. And tenants. Nothing more. We don't own the cabins we live in. We don't own anything here. Those two guys in there do. The two guys you were just about to punch."

I ran my hand through my hair and sighed. When he laid it all out like that, I could see his point. But still . . . "That still doesn't make it right," I said, the fight in me gone. "This is your home. Those people in there are your family. Jesus, Davo. I spent the last two days thinking about how much I don't want to leave, how bad I wanted to stay here, and it doesn't matter because you're not staying anyway." My eyes burned with tears I refused to cry. "It's all over and I don't get a say in it."

He stared at me, his chest rising and falling. "You want to stay?"

I scoffed and pulled at my hair. "How can I not? You . . ." God, was I going to say this?

"Fuck!" I yelled. I had to put my hands on my knees to try and catch my breath.

He touched my back. "Fergus?"

I stood up, my heart in my throat.

"'We are but a speck of dust in the time of this place.' That's what you said. Those words hit me so hard, Davo. And the stars at night . . . my god. We are tiny, insignificant in the scheme of the universe and infinite time." I wasn't making any sense. "So if none of it matters, if in the end we're just names in some forgotten history book god knows when from now, then I want to make my time count.

"You said out of the billions of years, how lucky you were to live at the same time as me. What are the fucking odds? I have nothing in Sydney. Nothing to go back to. Because I was meant to come here. I was meant to meet you, Davo. I was meant to stay." I had to blink back my tears. "And now none of it matters anyway because you're all leaving."

He crashed into me, wrapping his arms around me in a fierce hug. "Of course it matters, Fergus. My god, would you really stay?" He pulled back. "For real? For me?"

"Oh, here's Rocky," Gibbo said from behind us.

Davo and I broke apart, and Davo put his hand to his heart, a happy, bewildered look on his face.

Truck laughed and clapped my shoulder. "Thought you were gonna flatten him."

It took me a second to realise they were talking about me wanting to punch those two arseholes. I shook my head, my hand pressed to my forehead. "I've never hit anyone in my life. I'd have broken my hand for sure."

Bronnie and Junie both smiled as they found us as well. "You okay, Davo?" Junie asked.

Of course she'd notice something was off between us.

"Uh, yeah," he replied, breathless. "I think."

Then, of course, Gibbo and Truck looked between us. "What's going on?"

I tried to lick my lips—my mouth was too dry. Instead, I just shook my head and ran my hand through my hair. Davo let out a deep exhale. "Well, we were just discussing the possibility, maybe, of Fergus staying." His voice was tight, and when I finally risked eye contact, he grinned. "Right? You meant that?"

I scoffed. "Of course I did. Except for the fact that they're taking your town from you and none of you seem to care. So where would I even be staying? I mean, with you, but where?" I gestured to Davo. "And you'll be living away two weeks a month on some stupid fly-in, fly-out fucking contract. I mean, it's not a deal-breaker. I'm just trying to get my head around everything."

Davo was still grinning, looking at me with hearts in his eyes as I spoke, then he threw himself at me, almost knocking me over in one of his fierce hugs. "I can't believe you're not leaving. I don't want you to go," he whispered in my ear. "Please say you'll stay."

I nodded. "Yes."

He squeezed me harder, laughing, buzzing with excitement. Someone cleared their throat and we broke apart, but

Davo held onto my arm like he feared I'd disappear if he let me go.

Everyone else was looking at us all cutesy like they weren't just told by their bosses that they were all expendable, that their permanent status was all but over. They'd be living god knew where, working somewhere else, flying in and out all the damn time.

It was like I was missing something . . .

Oh god.

I peeled myself from Davo, taking it in turns to look at each of them. "You guys know something I don't. What am I missing?"

Davo was still grinning. "Sorry, I can't stop smiling." He even tried squishing his cheeks to stop. "You just made me the happiest guy. I'm just gonna need a minute." Then he laughed.

Okay, so he wasn't telling me. I looked at the others for some help.

"What am I missing?"

Gibbo and Creepy shrugged, then JC did, and Truck made a face. Junie sighed. "We have a plan," she said.

We have a plan.

Of course they did.

They all smiled, looking at each other. Bronnie clapped her hands together. "We got two years to pull it together."

I SAT in my cabin while Davo explained their plan. It'd been ten years in the making, and while they would have preferred another four or five years at Pannalego, two would just have to do.

"We always knew the contract here would end. They

always do. No mine stays in operation forever," he said. "We've been saving every cent. We make real good money, and living here costs us nothing. There is very little to buy. But we don't need anything, so we basically saved every cent."

I knew base contract rates for engineers in the mining sector, especially back ten years ago when they started, could earn up to one hundred and sixty thousand per year, maybe even more. Times that by ten years.

My head began to swim.

"You're doing the maths right now, aren't you?"

"I'm trying not to," I admitted. "Because I can't . . . I don't have anything close to that."

"You don't need it."

He said it so simply, so effortlessly. It wasn't making sense.

"I can sell my car," I said, stupidly. It was probably worth ten grand, tops. "And I can get a job here. It'll pay for . . . something. God, I'll have to tell my parents. My father will assume I'm being held captive, and if I ask them to sell my stuff, he'll think it's a ransom."

I had no idea what I could do. I was purely grasping at straws. I wanted to stay so bad, but the details, the realities, weren't so sweet. They had the money to make it work.

I didn't.

Davo knelt between my legs and cupped my face. "Fergus, look at me."

I met his eyes.

"Do you want to stay here?"

"More than anything." I nodded. "I didn't expect to come here and fall in love. But I met you, and you are *everything* I want. You are so perfectly right for me. You see the wonder in the world, and I need someone to remind me of that. You're smart and funny, and you're just everything I could ever need."

His eyes got impossibly blue and teary. "You love me?"

I said that, didn't I?

"I love you. I'm in love with you," I admitted. "When we made love the other night, I knew there was no going back for me."

His chin wobbled and he barked out a teary laugh. "My god. I love you too. Since the second I found you in the cool room on your first day here. You looked up at me like it was completely normal to be sitting in a fridge. You didn't care that I was wearing a skirt, and your copper hair and freckles. How could I not fall in love with you?"

I held his face, my forehead to his, and tried not to cry. I was so overwhelmed. "I'm staying. I don't know how I'll make anything work or how I'll earn any money, but it'd kill me if I had to leave you." I let out a shaky breath. "It scares me, if I'm being honest. How fast this is, how intense. How real it is."

"It is scary," he murmured. "But it is real, Ferg. And we'll be okay. You and me."

I nodded. "You and me."

He drew me in for a soft kiss. "I love you. And don't you worry about a thing. We've got it all worked out."

EPILOGUE

YANDIBAH BAY WAS A VERY small inlet town on the northwest coast of Western Australia. Off the main road, so it had been overlooked and forgotten, mostly. It hadn't been much more than a roadhouse with some camping sites, petrol bowsers, and cold drinks.

But the ocean sure was pretty, minus the great white sharks and the Irukandji jellyfish, of course.

I was used to all the things that tried to kill me now. Animals on land, animals in the sea, cyclones, and the heat.

Crazy to believe anyone would want to live here by choice. But I wouldn't want to live anywhere else.

I'd been over here for five years. I spent two years at Pannalego while the mine saw out its time. I absolutely loved living there. Loved it more than I thought I would.

And it took the full two years for the Grand Plan to come together. None of the permanent residents of Pannalego renewed their contract to transfer to the new mine. Well, except for Cookie. He went to the new mine, and no one blamed him. He said he had another ten years in him before he could retire and never have to worry about money again.

But everyone else was out of the mining industry. They'd all worked their arses off for twelve years and made a fortune. Davo was thirty-two, and for all intents and purposes, he retired on a shit tonne of money.

Free to do whatever he wanted. They all were. And what they wanted to do was buy the Yandibah Bay roadhouse.

They each had a new holiday cabin installed, all in a row like how they used to live in Pannalego, only this time they fronted the water. Ours was a two-bedroom cabin—our bedroom and a sewing room—complete with a little porch out the front for our rainbow spinner that spun forever in the sea breeze.

The other campsites were to be rented out to travellers and holidaymakers.

To be frank, they never bought the property to make money. They bought it to live in and to keep their little makeshift town together. But as it turned out, they got busy, and it was more like a roadhouse and a holiday park for travellers.

Junie and Bronnie ran the roadhouse. Bill and Truck were busy in the garage workshop, fixing and servicing all the travelling vehicles and caravans that stopped by.

Davo, along with Gibbo, JC, Creepy, and Chappy, all engineers and handymen to the bone, made it their mission to fix up the place—the guests' amenities, plumbing, roofing, the fences, the gardens, the pathways, the signs, a playground for kids—they were always mending or building something. And the place looked a million dollars.

Probably closer to five million. But no one was counting.

We had a communal BBQ area that we used every

Friday night, all sitting around and talking crap. Any guests were welcome to join us if they wanted. It wasn't exactly a terrible view, being right on the water, and the stories were always funny.

I'd been worried about not earning money or contributing my share, but I ended up getting two jobs. One at the regional council and one at the local newspaper. They just sorta fell in my lap. I'd told my old boss that I quit, making the department's decision on who to fire a lot easier. I told him my report didn't mean shit when private companies and governments were going to sway any findings in their own favour anyway.

But after I'd calmed down a bit and had more time on my hands than I knew what to do with, I finished my report. I submitted the paper to the council offices and submitted the introduction and conclusion in a letter format to the local newspaper.

And it got read by a lot of people. And the right people, apparently, because quite a few contacted me, keen to discuss.

My findings, to put it simply, were that no matter how much of a light the different industries brought into the region, which was incredibly important, it was the people who shone the brightest.

It would always come down to the people.

Always.

The council was impressed that I had a degree in human sciences and had worked in research across different fields, and they offered me work two days a week. Mostly research and report findings, but I could do it with my eyes closed.

After a long conversation with the editor of the newspaper, she offered me some copywriting work with an occasional opinion piece. It was purely work-from-home, two days a week.

Easy freaking peasy.

Life at Yandibah Bay was ridiculously laid back. We were in permanent holiday mode, and it was glorious.

Life with Davo was perfect.

Not always easy, and there were some adjustments way back in the beginning, but I'd never been happier.

I loved him more now, more every day.

He still wore his skirts, never ashamed to be his true self. Even with the guests and holidayers at the park. It was just accepted. The fact that he was muscular and ripped and wore old T-shirts and work boots probably made it confusing for some, but as soon as he smiled and helped whomever needed help, no one ever seemed to care.

He had more time to do more sewing now, and he'd made me a lot of pairs of shorts. Some were great for wearing in public. Some were not. Like the pairs that were so tight, it looked like I'd been poured into them. Or the pairs with the flap at the front so I didn't have to waste time taking them off. I could just pop the flap, pull my dick out, and lift his skirt.

"What's got you smiling?" Davo asked.

It was dark out. The autumn night was lovely and cool. Inside our cabin was warm and homey, perfect for just us. He'd finished cleaning up after dinner while I worked up the courage to show him what I'd ordered for him. I closed my laptop. "Thinking about you."

"Hm," he said. "Any particular part of me?" He swung his leg over my thighs and sat on my crotch, his skirt riding high. "Imagine if you were wearing those shorts I made. I could just pop the flap."

I laughed. "That's exactly what I was thinking about."

His eyes lit up. "Did you want to change into them?"

I pulled his chin down so I could kiss his lips. "*You* have a one-track mind."

"And you have the best dick." He pulled his skirt up a bit higher and rocked his hips. "So, really, it's your fault."

It was now or never.

God, Fergus. Just do it.

"So, I, er, I bought you something. It arrived today," I said. I shouldn't be nervous. This was Davo. No one on the planet understood me better than him.

"Oh? Like what?" His expression was both excited and wary. "And why are you nervous?"

I tapped his leg. "Turn around and face the table. Close your eyes."

He manoeuvred himself so he was facing the table but sitting on my lap. He covered his eyes with both hands and decided to grind a little. "Oh, this is good. We haven't done this position in a while."

I laughed, because of course he would think of that.

But then I took his gift out of my laptop bag and slid it onto the table in front of him. I buried my face against his back. "Before you open your eyes, I want you to know there's no pressure. I'm just putting this out there."

He was quiet for a second, confused. "Okay."

"Open your eyes."

I felt him freeze when he saw it, and then he sat side-on so he could see me. "Fergus?"

"It's a skirt pattern book."

He looked at the book, then at me. "No, it's a *Bridal* dressmaker's skirt pattern book."

I swallowed quickly. "I thought you might like to look through it," I said. "To get ideas. See if you like any of them."

He opened his mouth and closed it again, lightly touching the front of the book. "Fergus, I . . ."

"I figured they'd be complex and a lot of work, and you'd need to order in the right material, and it would take months and months to find the material you wanted, and even if it didn't happen for a year or two, that'd be okay if you wanted to wait, but I thought maybe you might want ideas, and there's a white tulle skirt on page forty-seven that I think would look amazing on you."

He pursed his lips together, far too quiet for my liking. But he turned to page forty-seven. The skirt was tulle, like a full-and-floofy princess style but maybe if she was a cool princess, even a bit slutty.

He nodded. "It's . . . it's actually really beautiful."

"But?"

"But there's just one thing you seemed to have forgotten, Ferg."

Christ. Was he mad?

"What's that?"

"The part where you ask me to marry you." He looked bewildered. "I mean, is that what this is? Are you even asking, or did you just think wedding skirts was a good idea for something different?"

I cupped the side of his face and looked into those blue, blue eyes. "David Senter," I whispered. "I want to spend my life with you. There is no one, in all the time on earth, in all the stars in the universe, I'd rather spend my life with but you. I would be honoured and humbled if you'd be my husband. I want to marry you. I want to be yours forever. Marry me, please. Choose your favourite skirt, take as long as you want to make it. When you're ready, we can plan a wedding. A small, private ceremony, on the beach, if you want—"

He kissed me soundly. "I can have something shipped in two days."

I laughed. "Is that a yes?"

"Of course, it's a yes!" He kissed me again. "My god, Fergus, yes. And the Cinderella-hooker skirt is perfect. Oh, that reminds me, we're looking after Hooker tomorrow. Bronnie asked. I said of course we would."

I laughed. "Of course."

"And Creepy's got that latest order on his website he needed your help with shipping costs or something."

"Oh, he sold the big croc sculpture? That's awesome."

He smiled, pressing his forehead to mine. "You sure you want to marry me?"

"Never been surer about anything in my life." I took his face in both my hands. "I love you. I wouldn't change a single thing about you. Or our lives together. Except maybe my ring on your finger."

"And mine on yours," he said, kissing me softly.

THE END

Thank you for reading

ABOUT THE AUTHOR

N.R. Walker is an Australian author, who loves her genre of gay romance. She loves writing and spends far too much time doing it, but wouldn't have it any other way.

She is many things: a mother, a wife, a sister, a writer. She has pretty, pretty boys who live in her head, who don't let her sleep at night unless she gives them life with words.

She likes it when they do dirty, dirty things... but likes it even more when they fall in love.

She used to think having people in her head talking to her was weird, until one day she happened across other writers who told her it was normal.

She's been writing ever since...

ALSO BY N.R. WALKER

Reindeer Games

The Dichotomy of Angels

Throwing Hearts

Pieces of You - Missing Pieces #1

Pieces of Me - Missing Pieces #2

Pieces of Us - Missing Pieces #3

Lacuna

Tic-Tac-Mistletoe

Bossy

Code Red

Dearest Milton James

Dearest Malachi Keogh

Christmas Wish List

Code Blue

TITLES IN AUDIO:

Cronin's Key

Cronin's Key II

Cronin's Key III

Red Dirt Heart

Red Dirt Heart 2

Red Dirt Heart 3

Red Dirt Heart 4

The Weight Of It All

Switched

The Hate You Drink

Pieces of You

Pieces of Me

Pieces of Us

Tic-Tac-Mistletoe

Lacuna

Bossy

Code Red

Learning to Feel

Dearest Milton James

Dearest Malachi Keogh

Three's Company

Christmas Wish List

Series Collections (as ebook box sets):

Red Dirt Heart Series

Turning Point Series

Thomas Elkin Series

Spencer Cohen Series

Imago Series

Blind Faith Series

Free Reads:

Sixty Five Hours

Learning to Feel

His Grandfather's Watch (And The Story of Billy and Hale)
The Twelfth of Never (Blind Faith 3.5)
Twelve Days of Christmas (Sixty Five Hours Christmas)
Best of Both Worlds

TRANSLATED TITLES:

ITALIAN

Fiducia Cieca (Blind Faith)
Attraverso Questi Occhi (Through These Eyes)
Preso alla Sprovvista (Blindside)
Il giorno del Mai (Blind Faith 3.5)
Cuore di Terra Rossa Serie (Red Dirt Heart Series)
Natale di terra rossa (Red dirt Christmas)
Intervento di Retrofit (Elements of Retrofit)
A Chiare Linee (Clarity of Lines)
Senso D'appartenenza (Sense of Place)
Spencer Cohen Serie (including Yanni's Story)
Punto di non Ritorno (Point of No Return)
Punto di Rottura (Breaking Point)
Punto di Partenza (Starting Point)
Imago (Imago)
Il desiderio di un soldato (A Soldier's Wish)
Scambiato (Switched)
Galassie e Oceani (Galaxies and Oceans)

FRENCH

Confiance Aveugle (Blind Faith)

A travers ces yeux: Confiance Aveugle 2 (Through These Eyes)

Aveugle: Confiance Aveugle 3 (Blindside)

À Jamais (Blind Faith 3.5)

Cronin's Key Series

Au Coeur de Sutton Station (Red Dirt Heart)

Partir ou rester (Red Dirt Heart 2)

Faire Face (Red Dirt Heart 3)

Trouver sa Place (Red Dirt Heart 4)

Le Poids de Sentiments (The Weight of It All)

Un Noël à la sauce Henry (A Very Henry Christmas)

Une vie à Refaire (Switched)

Evolution (Evolved)

Galaxies & Océans

Qui Trouve, Garde (Finders Keepers)

Sens Dessus Dessous (Upside Down)

GERMAN

Flammende Erde (Red Dirt Heart)

Lodernde Erde (Red Dirt Heart 2)

Sengende Erde (Red Dirt Heart 3)

Ungezähmte Erde (Red Dirt Heart 4)

Vier Pfoten und ein bisschen Zufall (Finders Keepers)

Ein Kleines bisschen Versuchung (The Weight of It All)

Ein Kleines Bisschen Fur Immer (A Very Henry Christmas)

Weil Leibe uns immer Bliebt (Switched)

Drei Herzen eine Leibe (Three's Company)

Über uns die Sterne, zwischen uns die Liebe (Galaxies and Oceans)

Unnahbares Herz (Blind Faith 1)

Sehendes Herz (Blind Faith 2)

Hoffnungsvolles Herz (Blind Faith 3)

Verträumtes Herz (Blind Faith 3.5)

Thomas Elkin: Verlangen in neuem Design

THAI

Sixty Five Hours (Thai translation)

Finders Keepers (Thai translation)

SPANISH

Sesenta y Cinco Horas (Sixty Five Hours)

Código Rojo (Code Red)

Código Azul (Code Blue)

Queridísimo Milton James

Queridísimo Malachi Keogh

El Peso de Todo (The Weight of it All)

Tres Muérdagos en Raya: Serie Navidad en Hartbridge

Lista De Deseos Navideños: Serie Navidad en Hartbridge

CHINESE

Blind Faith

CPSIA information can be obtained
at www.ICGtesting.com
Printed in the USA
BVHW061333060522
636303BV00003B/254